SIREN
Publishing

Slick Rock 1

Ménage Everlasting

BECCA VAN

DELIVERANCE

Deliverance

When Lilac Primrose arrives in Slick Rock, Colorado she thinks she's jumped from the frying pan into the fire.

Having escaped a hostage, cult style life at the tender age of fifteen, and then making a life for herself independently from anyone else, Lilac wants to run again when she notices the prevalent, unusual relationships around town. However, since she has good morals and has signed a lease contract, she stays put.

Retired Marines, Wilder, Cree, and Nash Sheffield have only recently moved to Slick Rock and are about to start new jobs as deputy sheriffs. The moment they see Lilac, they're mesmerized and are determined to court her.

When Lilac begins to remember more of her past and finds out she's not who she thinks she is, she seeks the help of the deputies and sheriffs.

Lilac ends up in danger and facing her past head on, but this time she's not sure she'll be able to escape.

Genre: Contemporary, Ménage a Trois/Quatre, Western/Cowboys
Length: 58,209 words

DELIVERANCE

Slick Rock 17

Becca Van

Siren Publishing, Inc.
www.SirenPublishing.com

DEDICATION

To all my loyal readers. You're forever in my heart. Thank you so much for your continued support.

Love, Becca xxoo.

ABOUT THE AUTHOR

My name is Becca Van. I live in Australia with my wonderful hubby of many years, as well as my two children.

I read my first romance, which I found in the school library, at the age of thirteen and haven't stopped reading them since. It is so wonderful to know that love is still alive and strong when there seems to be so much conflict in the world.

I dreamed of writing my own book one day, but unfortunately, didn't follow my dream for many years. But once I started I knew writing was what I wanted to continue doing.

I love to escape from the world and curl up with a good romance, to see how the characters unfold and conflict is dealt with. I have read many books and love all facets of the romance genre, from historical to erotic romance. I am a sucker for a happy ending.

For all titles by Becca Van, please visit
www.bookstrand.com/becca-van

DELIVERANCE

Slick Rock 17

BECCA VAN
Copyright © 2018

Prologue

"Are you serious?" Lilac asked Delta before looking at the contract in her hand. She glanced over at Enya to see the other woman was just as surprised as she was. Enya was also holding a sheaf of papers.

"Deadly serious," Delta signed and Major, one of her fiancés, spoke on her behalf.

"You want Enya and I to buy into the diner and become equal partners?" Lilac asked a little hoarsely. She couldn't believe her boss's generosity. She, Enya, and the other women had only been working for Delta for a few short weeks.

Delta smiled and nodded. "Yes."

"Why?" Lilac swallowed around the emotional constriction in her throat. "Why would you do this?"

"Because after what happened, I've realized that there are more important things in life than just work. I love cooking for the people who come into the diner, but I also want to spend more time with my guys."

When Delta finished signing and Major stopped talking, the big handsome man had a wide grin on his face. Major shifted his gaze from Lilac and Enya, and when he looked at Delta, his eyes were so full of love, Lilac felt as if she was being voyeuristic on a private moment.

Lilac glanced at Enya and the other woman gave her a slight nod as if encouraging her to say yes.

"Are you sure?" Lilac asked, worried that this wasn't real.

She'd dreamed of owning her own place from a young age, and while she'd worked hard toward that goal after she'd managed to escape those crazy people's clutches, she'd never expected it to happen. Delta was offering her a chance of realizing that dream even if it was as a part owner. She'd be stupid to pass up such a wonderful opportunity.

"Thank you, Delta. I accept." Lilac blinked back tears of gratitude. Her heart was so full of emotion it was painful.

"I accept, too," Enya said and rushed over to give Delta a hug. When she drew back, Lilac saw tears coursing down the other woman's face. She knew exactly how she felt because she was still struggling to keep the tears stinging her eyes at bay, too. "Thank you."

"You're both very welcome," Delta replied.

"This is the reason you've scheduled us all to work alternate hours, isn't it?" Lilac asked.

"Yes." Delta nodded and smiled.

"When do you need the money by?" Enya asked.

"There's no hurry. You can pay me a little each week or whenever you can afford to."

Lilac was still having trouble accepting Delta's generosity, and while she knew there was nothing nefarious about the offer, she'd learned to be very wary. However, there was nothing sinister with the proposal or the contract. She'd read it over before entering the kitchen. Delta had left the papers stuck to the outside of the cupboard she and Enya used to hide their purses in while they were working.

"I have the money," Lilac said. "I'd like to give it to you as soon as possible. Is a bank check all right with you? Or do you prefer cash?"

"Whatever you want is fine, Lilac. I'm so glad to have you and Enya as partners. I know we're going to make this place the best diner in Colorado."

Lilac was of the same opinion, and by the excited look on Enya's face, she agreed, too.

The smile slid from Enya's lips. "I only have half the money in savings."

Delta waved her hand in the air. "I don't care how long it takes for you to pay for your share in the business. That's not important. I'm just happy to have you both as partners and friends."

Lilac's cheeks began to hurt from smiling so much. All the hard work she'd put into her education and then doing her best while cooking as head chef in New York City was finally paying off.

She'd spent ten years of her childhood in absolute hell and wondered if the penance she'd already paid had led her to this once-in-a-lifetime chance.

She just hoped that nothing and no one tried to take it away from her.

She'd spent the last ten years of her life looking over her shoulder, hoping that she never had to face any of those monsters again.

A shiver of apprehension ran up her spine, but she pushed it aside. Nothing was going to stand in the way of her career. Cooking was the only thing that had kept her sane, and if that was taken away from her, she wasn't sure she'd survive.

Chapter One

"Fucking cunt." Virgil couldn't believe that bitch had slipped away from him again.

He forced a smile to his face as he entered the motel.

"Welcome to the Slick Rock Motel, how can I help you?"

Virgil eyed the smiling young woman over and licked his lips. When the welcoming smile left her mouth and she took a step back, he hid the smirk wanting to form and met her gaze.

"I'd like to book a room please?"

"How long will you be staying?"

"I'm not sure yet. I'm on vacation and want to do as many touristy things as I can." The woman handed over some paperwork and after reading through it and filling in the necessities, she asked, "Will you be paying with cash or credit card?"

"Cash." He pulled his wallet from his pocket and handed over enough money for a week, hoping that was all the time he'd need for what he wanted to do. If not, he'd pay day by day.

"You're in room ten, if you need anything don't hesitate to call reception. The desk is manned at all times."

"Thanks." Virgil took the key the woman had placed on the desk and hurried out the door. As he walked toward his room, that bitch flashed across his mind.

He'd been trying to find Lilac for nigh on ten years. It didn't matter that he'd partaken of the other women and girls his father kept under lock and key. He was obsessed with Lilac Primrose, and he wouldn't give up until he'd found her. The old man had died a few years back, and ever since he'd taken over the running of the place and even before that, he'd been searching for that slut.

He'd hit pay dirt a few months back when he'd taken time away from his home to see the sights of New York City. When he'd first seen the picture of the renowned chef in the window of Rembrandt's Restaurant, he had nearly died with shock.

She was the one who had gotten away and while he'd looked for her everywhere, he hadn't found her. When he'd spied that photo, he knew fate was playing a hand in guiding him in the right direction and he'd entered the swanky restaurant then and there, and booked a table. The need to have her under him had never gone away and the hunger had surged through his blood, leaving him shaken, excited, and as hard as hell.

Yet, she'd somehow managed to escape him again. He had no idea how she knew he was in town, but guessed she'd seen him without his knowledge. The bitch had disappeared without a trace. He'd never forget the uproar that had ensued in the kitchen of the restaurant that night. Diners had ended up waiting way too long for the meals they'd ordered. The manager had tried to pacify angry customers, but most of the people had walked out in disgust. He'd hung around, and though he figured the meal he'd eaten wasn't up to the usual standards, it hadn't been bad and he hadn't had to pay a dime.

His dearly departed father hadn't been as smart as Virgil, but at least the old bastard had conceded to let him attend college. All the welfare money his dad collected on behalf of the other members of the cult, and the government handouts for fostering those sluts and the teenage boys, had paved his way to getting his degree in IT. Virgil had always had an affinity with computers and studying had ramped up his skills. It had taken a few years to teach himself, but he was also a skilled and avid hacker.

Even though he still lived at that rundown commune his father had set up, Virgil ruled with an iron fist. Any time he clicked his fingers

he'd have the women running to service him. They were too cowardly
to refuse because if they didn't, those bitches knew there would be
hell to pay. He smiled with satisfaction. Virgil was sitting pretty, and
other than making sure the money kept flowing, he hardly ever had to
lift a finger.

As soon as he'd arrived back home he'd ordered Fleur to his bed,
and while he'd been slaking his lust with the biddable bitch, he'd
imagined he was fucking Lilac. He didn't remember wrapping his
hands around her neck and squeezing the life out of her, but he did
remember the ecstasy that had ripped through his body. When he'd
finally come back to himself, it was to find Fleur staring at the ceiling
with unseeing eyes. Although Virgil knew he should have felt guilty
for taking a life, he didn't give a shit. He didn't care about any of the
people living on his land. All he cared about was raking in the money
the government paid out.

It had been hard work to get rid of the body in the dead of night,
but he hadn't had a choice. He could have ordered one of the other
guys to do his dirty work for him, but he didn't trust any of them as
far as he could kick them. He'd waited until three in the morning to
make his move and after checking to make sure no one was up and
about, he'd wrapped that bitch up in a sheet and carried her out to his
truck.

Virgil had driven to the far edge of his land, dug a deep grave, and
then dumped the bitch in the hole. He'd been sweating and exhausted,
but at least no one had known what he'd done.

The next morning he'd gone about his usual routine as if nothing
had happened. That was until Rose had noticed Fleur was gone. When
she started asking questions, Virgil had acted puzzled and worried
like the rest of the guys, and after a thorough search of the place he'd
started cursing. He'd told everyone that there would be no food until
Fleur was found, and then he'd gone and hidden in his office.

Grant and Warren had informed him that Fleur was gone and he'd
planted the seed that the bitch had escaped. Word had spread, and the

tension had eased. Being the nice person he was, he'd ordered dinner to be made and let everyone eat their fill. Things had gone back to normal.

Whenever Virgil left the cult for some time out, he left Grant and Warren in charge. Those two assholes were just as hedonistic as he was, and though he didn't care about how many women they fucked while he was gone, he made sure they didn't do any permanent damage. He was their god, and whatever he said was law. There was no way in hell he was letting those bastards harm his regular fucks.

He rubbed at the back of his neck and glanced at his watch. He'd just booked into the motel on the edge of town, and while he wanted to make sure the Lilac Primrose he'd found was the woman he was looking for, he was tired. He'd spent the better part of two days sitting in his truck as he drove from Werner, Minnesota, to Slick Rock, Colorado. Decided on his plan of action, he picked up the phone and ordered room service. Tomorrow would be here before he knew it, and then he was going to scope out the town and find that bitch.

Even if it took him until he was old and gray, Virgil was going to get what he wanted.

Lilac Primrose under him as he fucked her hard, and then he was going to kill her.

* * * *

"It's so good to see you." Major Porter shoved from the chair behind his desk and hurried over to his three cousins.

"That it is," Wilder Sheffield, one of Major's cousins, replied and pulled him into a hug.

"How the hell are you, Major?" Cree asked when his cousin turned from his brother toward him.

"Well." Major grinned as he slapped Cree on the back while they hugged. "Happy."

"You look happy, cousin." Nash grinned and gave Major a bear hug before releasing the big man.

"Come have a seat." Major indicated the chair in front of his desk and pointed to the spares along the wall. "How long has it been?"

"It's been too damn long," Wilder answered as he sat across from the desk.

Major hurried around his desk and took his own seat again.

"How's the rest of the family?" Nash asked as he and Cree positioned their chairs on either side of Wilder.

"All good. Ace and Rocco are scouting the area for a house to buy. We're thinking of expanding the ranch. Our cattle sales are through the roof, so we decided while things were going so well we'd add to our land."

"That's great news." Cree smiled.

"How is Delta, and when do we get to meet her?" Wilder asked.

"She's working right now, but she should be home by three." Major grinned. "She asked two other women to become part owners of the diner, and luckily they accepted. Our woman wanted to spend more time with me, Ace, and Rocco."

"I know we're here for the engagement party, but have you set a date for the wedding yet?"

Major nodded. "We're getting hitched on the fourth of July."

"That's only a couple of months away," Wilder said. "I can tell by how you talk about her that you love her and how damn happy you are. I'm glad you've found the perfect woman for you three."

"She loves us just as much," Major said. "We're lucky to have found her." He cleared his throat. "So how long are you guys planning on staying?"

"Permanently," Nash answered with a smile.

"'Bout fucking time." Major chuckled. "I'm glad you all decided it was time to get out of the military."

"Yeah," Wilder sighed. "We've done our duty and decided it was high time to settle down."

"We discussed moving away from Denver a few years back, but we weren't ready then," Cree explained.

"And you are now?" Major quirked an eyebrow.

"We are," the Sheffield men answered simultaneously.

"When you told us how protective the men were of the women and kids here, that just made sense to us," Wilder said.

"And being able to have one woman to share between us was the clincher." Cree shrugged.

Nash nodded. "When we heard about the polyamorous relationships and how accepting the locals were..."

"Yeah, I hear ya." Major grinned. "Have you decided what you want to do now that you're retired Marines?"

Wilder cleared his throat. "We were hoping that you'd hire us on, cousin."

"You were, were you?" Major sank back into his chair and shook his head. "I can't see you three being happy ranching. I think you'd be more suited to law enforcement."

Wilder glanced at Cree and Nash with a frown. When his identical brothers nodded, he sighed.

Major sat forward and leaned his elbows on his desk, waiting patiently for his cousins to answer.

"Major's right," Cree said.

Nash nodded. "I agree."

"Hold on a second." Wilder held up his hand and turned his gaze back to Major. "Have you been checking up on us?"

"No. Why the hell would you ask that?" Major frowned.

"Because we just happened to have sat the written and physical tests required to become deputies." Nash grinned.

"You did?"

"We did," Cree answered.

"Well, well, well. What a coincidence." Major said.

"There's only one problem." Wilder bent forward and rested his elbows on his knees.

"What's that?" Major asked.

"We don't even know if there's any need for more deputies in Slick Rock." Nash scrubbed a hand down his face.

"If I remember rightly, Sheriff Luke Sun-Walker was bitching about how fast this town was growing and his need for more men." Major tapped his chin. "I could set up a meeting with him if you'd like."

"We don't need to you hold our hands, cousin." Wilder scowled.

"I know that." Major smirked. "How about I take you into town so you can talk to the sheriff."

Wilder stood, nodded, and glanced at his watch. "No time like the present, but we'll follow you. It's almost lunch time, and after hearing you, Rocco, and Ace rave over what a wonderful chef your woman is, I think we should see if you're right."

"Asshole," Major said good-naturedly. "You just want to get a look at my woman."

Nash chuckled as he followed Wilder toward the office door. "You have us pegged, cousin. We can meet you at the diner after we've finished with the sheriff. Save us a seat."

"Will do," Major said. "Rocco and Ace were going to meet me there for lunch anyway."

Cree paused on the verandah of the ranch house to meet Major's gaze. "You'd better make sure you get us a big table then."

"I'll get a booth. We should fit okay since they're supposed to fit about ten people."

"It'll be a squeeze, but we'll make do." Wilder opened the driver's door to the truck and got in. Cree sat in the front passenger seat and Nash got in the back.

Major hopped into his truck and headed to town. He was eager to see the love of his life.

* * * *

"So you're Major's, Rocco's, and Ace's cousins?" Sheriff Luke Sun-Walker asked.

"We are," Wilder answered. "We retired from the Marines about a month ago, and since we want to stay in Slick Rock permanently we need jobs. We asked Major to hire us on as ranch hands, and while we have nothing against hard farm work and would probably enjoy a change, being in law enforcement would suit us better."

"Why is that?"

"We hate seeing injustice." Cree shifted in his seat. "We like protecting the innocent. We joined up as soon as we had our high school diplomas and served ten years in the Marines. However, if you don't have a need for more deputies that's okay."

Luke shook his head. "Slick Rock is growing so fast. I can't believe how my hometown is booming. You probably saw all the new housing estates close to town. More shops have opened, and the population has more than doubled in the last five years. The surrounding towns and county have exploded, too."

"So, what are you saying?" Wilder asked.

"I need more men. You'll need to sit the written exam, and while I know y'all are more than up to the task physically, you'll have to go through the process," Luke explained.

Wilder nodded, bent down, and opened the small duffle bag he'd brought with him and dug into it. He pulled out a large yellow envelope, stood, and then moved closer to the desk. "We have everything you need right here."

Luke opened the envelope and pulled the papers out. He read over each page before meeting each of their gazes again. "You've already passed the tests."

"We have." Cree grinned.

"We've also taken out a short-term lease on a house in one of the new estates." Nash crossed his arms over his chest.

"Did you tell Major this? He, Rocco, and Ace are going to be over the moon that you'll be staying."

Wilder shook his head and then nodded. "We told him we wanted to move here permanently, but we haven't had the chance to tell him we've already leased a place."

"I'll need to run a background check on y'all, but I don't think there'll be any problems. When can you start?"

"Today's Thursday. If you can give us the weekend to finish unpacking and setting things up, we'll be ready to start on Monday." Cree glance at his brothers and they nodded.

"I'll do the check and let you know within half an hour." Luke rose.

"We're meeting the others at the diner for lunch," Wilder explained as he shook Luke's hand.

"I'll be over as soon as I have the results." Luke shook Cree's and then Nash's hands. "If everything checks out, are you all okay with starting on the afternoon shift?"

"We are," Nash replied.

"Good. I'll see you at the diner then."

"Thanks for everything, Luke," Wilder said as he and his brothers headed toward the door.

"It should be me thanking you." Luke grinned. "I didn't really want to go to all the trouble of advertising and interviewing. I don't have enough time."

"So it's a win-win all round." Nash nodded.

"It is," Luke said. "Be here at 1300 Monday. I'll have your badges and weapons ready. After y'all fill in the necessary paperwork you can start patrolling."

"We're looking forward to it, boss." Cree smirked.

"Me, too," Luke replied and then waved as Wilder, Cree, and Nash headed out.

"I can't wait for lunch"—Nash patted his stomach—"I'm starving."

"What happened to the last diner owner?" Wilder asked as he and his identical brothers followed Luke out of the office.

"She wanted to retire and decided to sell up," Luke said just before he entered Damon's office and waved before closing the door.

* * * *

"I can't believe how busy this place is," Cree said as he glanced about the diner. When he spied Major, Rocco, and Ace in a booth at the far end, he wended his way toward their cousins and scooted along the bench seat. "This place is hopping."

"It was always one of the places to be in town," Major said.

Rocco nodded. "The diner and the hotel."

Cree reached across to the table to shake Rocco's and Ace's hands. "Good to see your ugly mugs again."

"Yours, too." Ace offered his hand to Nash and then Major.

"What I can't believe," Cree began, "is how much Slick Rock has changed. We passed through here a few years back on the way home to Denver."

"It hasn't changed so much. It's just become bigger and busier." Rocco leaned back in the booth seat.

"Here you go," a young woman said as she placed mugs of coffee in front of Wilder, Cree, and Nash.

"Thanks, honey," Nash said.

"There's so much atmosphere here now." Wilder took a sip of coffee as he glanced around. "There is so much happiness and love, it's almost sickening."

"That's jealousy talking, Bro. We know you want what Major, Rocco, and Ace have just like Cree and I do." Nash frowned. "Or have you changed your mind?"

"Hell no!"

"Welcome to The Diner. My name is Cindy, and I'll be your server for the day. Are you ready to order?"

"What would you recommend, Cindy?" Cree winked and smiled at the young waitress.

Wilder hid his smirk when their server blushed. She was pretty but way too young for him and his brothers. Not that he was attracted to the young woman in any way.

"Today's specials are clam chowder with tuna melt mustard toasted sandwiches, tenderloin club sandwich, roast beef and vegetables, chicken parmesan, pulled pork sliders, as well as BBQ and Tennessee ribs, sirloin steak, as well as what's on the menu."

"I'll have the steak with fries and salad," Cree said.

"The chowder sounds good to me." Wilder smiled.

"I'll have the BBQ ribs with fries and salad, thanks," Nash ordered.

Major, Rocco, and Ace ordered the steak with peppercorn gravy.

"Do you want anything else to drink, or would you like more coffee?" Cindy asked.

"Coffee, thanks, hon," Wilder replied and everyone else nodded.

"Coming right up." Cindy hurried away with their order.

Luke and the other sheriff, Damon Osborn, entered the diner and added to the order before coming to sit with Cree, his brothers, and his cousins.

"What did you all order?" Luke asked as he sat across from Cree, Wilder, and Nash. It was a tight fit with eight tall, muscular men, but they managed to squeeze in. Damon sat at Luke's side and reached across to shake all their hands in greeting.

After they all replied, Cree asked the question uppermost in his mind. "So, did we check out?"

"You did." Luke grinned. "Welcome aboard the Slick Rock Sheriff's Department."

"You're starting work already?" Major grinned. "Do you have somewhere to stay? You can stay at the ranch if you want."

"We've already leased and moved into a place," Nash explained. "We still have a few boxes to unpack and set the place up how we want it, but we're here to stay."

"Fucking A." Ace nodded. "What made y'all want to move here?"

Wilder shifted in his seat. "We could hear how happy y'all were when we spoke on the phone last. We'd just completed our last tour and decided it was time to retire. It took us a month to get everything cleared away and sorted, as well as sit the tests, but here we are."

Nash leaned forward and said quietly, "We've shared a woman between us a time or two, as well, and couldn't believe how exciting and right it felt. We're closer than normal siblings since we're triplets, and we've always been attracted to the same women."

Cree set his coffee cup down. "We talked about finding a woman to share but didn't think it was possible since it wasn't the norm. When you called and told us you were all engaged to the same woman, we couldn't stay away."

"Just make sure you three are in this for the right reasons." Luke pointed at them. "We don't take kindly to guys stringing a female on and breaking her heart."

Wilder scowled at Luke. "We would *never* do such a thing. We're ready to settle down and have kids. The women we were with knew the score. They just wanted a night of fun so they could tell their friends they'd fucked a Marine."

Luke held his hands up in a placating gesture. "I didn't mean to offend. I just wanted to know you were here for the right reasons."

"We are," Nash said.

"Good. I'm glad that's settled." Luke smirked.

Cree sucked in a ragged breath when he noticed a beautiful white-blonde-haired woman come out from the back of the diner. He held his breath when she walked around the other side of the serving counter and took a seat on one of the stools. His heart flipped in his chest and his cock twitched in his pants. When his lungs began to burn, he released the air and sucked in another breath. "Who is that?"

"Who?" Damon asked as he glanced over his shoulder.

"The gorgeous blonde," Cree answered.

"Which one?" Damon turned to meet Cree's gaze, but Cree couldn't take his eyes off the sexy woman.

"What do you mean, which one?" He finally managed to drag his gaze from the blonde to look at Damon.

Luke chuckled. "If you haven't noticed, Cree, there is more than one blonde in here right now."

"The one with the white hair sitting at the counter."

"That's one of the owners. Her name is Lilac Primrose." Damon smirked.

"Are you yanking my chain?" Cree asked incredulously.

"No. That's her name. Lilac is a part owner of the diner with Delta and Enya," Major explained.

Cree wondered if her parents had been hippies or high on drugs when they'd named their baby girl, but as he stared at her, he thought the name fit. He'd seen her pale violet-colored eyes when she'd walked around the counter and figured her folks had named her after the color of her eyes.

"That is one beautiful piece of womanhood," Nash whispered.

"She's the sexiest fucking woman I've ever seen." Wilder sighed.

Cree turned his gaze to his brother and quirked an eyebrow in question. He rubbed his hands together with anticipated excitement. Moving closer to their cousins after getting out of the military had been a big decision, but now that he and his brothers were here, he knew their decision had been the right one.

They'd spent the last ten years serving their country and fighting wars. Now it was time to settle down and start a family. Cree had a feeling that Lilac was the woman he and his brothers had been waiting for.

Chapter Two

Lilac shivered when the hair on her nape stood on end. She froze with the spoon halfway to her mouth, trying to decide whether she should turn around and see who was watching her.

She'd been enjoying the clam chowder, but she dropped the spoon back into the bowl when her stomach began to churn. She was scared to look around and find out who was watching her just in case it was one of the monsters she'd spent ten years of her life with.

"Are you all right, Lilac?" Enya asked as she restocked the dessert display case.

"Yes. Just a little tired."

"I know how you feel," Enya said and sighed with tiredness after closing the glass sliding doors on the refrigerated case.

"Oh. Sorry. I shouldn't be whining when I know you've been up since four making all those delicious-looking muffins, cakes, and pies."

"You work just as hard as Delta and I do." Enya smiled. "You did the late shift last night and you're back here already. Plus, you're often up with me helping with the baking. I don't know how keep going."

Lilac shrugged. She didn't mind the long hours because she loved what she did. However, not being able to sleep through the night without nightmares plaguing her was getting a bit much.

"Are you having trouble sleeping?" Enya asked.

Lilac nodded. "A bit."

"If you ever need someone to talk to, I'm here. Okay?"

"Thank you." Lilac lowered her gaze back to her lunch, and though she tried to ignore that "being watched" feeling, she was too scared not to know who was staring at her. She turned sideways on her stool as she sipped her unsweetened iced tea and glanced about the room.

Her heart skipped a beat and her breath backed up in her lungs when she spotted three big men gazing at her. Her heart flipped in her chest and then slammed against her sternum. They all looked identical with black hair and green eyes, and they looked big all over. Even while they were sitting down, she could tell they were tall and their shoulders were so broad they were all touching. They were very muscular, too, and she wondered if they were gym junkies, but it was their handsome faces—the scruff on their jaws—that had her squirming in her seat. She quickly looked away, turned back to her lunch, and stirred the chowder with the spoon.

"You need to eat that." Enya pointed to her bowl. "I'll bet you didn't even take any time to eat breakfast. Did you?"

"No."

"You're paler than normal, Lilac. You need to eat more so you don't get sick. You don't want to pass out like Delta did, do you?"

"No." Lilac sighed and lifted the spoon to her mouth. She'd been enjoying her lunch until she felt eyes on her. Now, because she was so aware of those three handsome, identical men, the chowder tasted like cardboard. Nonetheless, she knew Enya was right. She needed to keep up her strength.

Food had been the only constant in her life, and while she could have turned away from cooking after having to cook for those horrible people all the time, it was all she knew. And she liked being able to make up delicious dishes for others to enjoy.

Even though she'd been free and virtually on her own since she was fifteen years old, she liked that she was finally making friends again. When she'd first landed in Slick Rock, she'd thought she'd ended up in another living nightmare. If it hadn't been for the fact that she'd signed a three-month lease, Lilac would have hightailed it out of town as soon as she saw the unusual relationships. Thankfully, she'd had a binding contract and she'd been able to see that the people in this growing rural town weren't anything like the monsters she'd lived with.

She'd watched Major, Rocco, and Ace intently while they'd courted Delta and had figured out the men in this town were nothing like those assholes in the cult. She'd finally been able to relax and concentrate on her passion of cooking. Yet Lilac had a feeling she would always be looking over her shoulder.

One of the reasons she'd left NYC was because she'd seen that bastard's son walking down the street as if he didn't have a care in the world.

Lilac had put a letter under the door to the Bemidji Police Station when she'd been fifteen years old, just after she'd escaped, but nothing had been done. There had been no write up in the local papers, no reports on arrests. She had no idea how those people had talked their way out of the situation, but she guessed they had, since none of them had been arrested. She'd wondered if the local law had been paid to turn a blind eye to what was going on in their own county. For all she knew, the sheriff may have been helping them kidnap children from their homes.

She'd wanted to take some of the other girls with her when she'd managed to get away, but she'd been scared of revealing her plans since she had no idea who she could trust and who she couldn't. She'd learned not to trust anyone, and although she'd been living with the other girls for years, she hadn't really known them. Nor had they'd known her. That wasn't a surprise, but maybe if she'd known how they felt about the way they were living, she might have tried to talk them into coming with her. However, she was too scared to trust anyone just in case the other girls would betray her. It had just been too damn risky. So Lilac had kept her mouth shut and waited for the opportunity to leave Werner, Minnesota.

She'd pilfered small quantities of nonperishable food which she'd hidden under some loose floorboards in her room and kept in a plastic container so the mice couldn't get to it. What she hated to do, but had been necessary, was steal money. It hadn't bothered her to take the food since she and the other girls were the ones who cooked it and ended up getting barely enough to sustain them. She'd felt so guilty taking the money meant to buy supplies, but if she hadn't, she wouldn't have been able to buy a bus ticket when she'd walked from Werner to Bemidji.

Lilac had never been so scared in her life. She'd had to duck off the road whenever a car had come along, terrified that she'd been discovered as missing and that the cult members had been out looking for her. She'd kept her hair covered with a hooded sweatshirt and her face in shadows, praying the whole time she'd been standing at the side of the Bemidji bus lines building for the time to pass faster, so she could buy a ticket out of Minnesota and get away.

Her heart had been racing the whole time, and even though she'd been cold, she'd also been covered in a fine sheen of sweat. However, it had been a clean getaway.

Lilac had only been fifteen years old and scared shitless as she'd traveled alone toward New York City, but once her decision had been made there was no going back.

Ever.

She'd been lucky so far and hoped her luck held out, but after seeing the cult leader's son, Virgil, walking down the street toward her restaurant, Lilac didn't think she'd ever feel safe again.

She'd been plagued with guilt because she'd been on her way to work, and when she'd seen Virgil, she had ducked into a shop across the road from the restaurant and watched. When he'd entered her place of work she knew she couldn't stay. There was no way in hell she was ever going back to Werner. So instead of heading into work like she was supposed to, Lilac had hailed a cab back to her one-bedroom bedsit and packed the few belongings she'd had. Although it meant losing her bond by breaking her lease, she hadn't really cared. All she'd cared about was getting out of New York City quickly.

She'd caught a cab to the closest train station and hopped on the first train. It had taken her over a week to get to Denver hopping from one train to the next and she'd been so exhausted, she'd booked into a room at a cheap motel. The next morning she'd bought a bus ticket and ridden the coach to the end of the line.

Lilac hadn't known what to do when she realized that another bus wasn't due to back for another week. Her mind had been in turmoil as she walked along the main street of town. She'd been so tired and hungry, she knew she needed to rest and had decided to book into a motel or someplace that leased rooms. However, when she'd seen the for-lease signs in the window of the local real estate office, she'd changed her mind.

Leases were much cheaper in Slick Rock than they had been in New York, and when she'd been working, she'd lived frugally. Her frugalness had paid off because when Delta had asked her and Enya to become part owners in the diner with her, she'd been able to give her all the money in cash.

Lilac blinked as she came back to the present. She couldn't believe she'd eaten all her chowder whilst lost in introspection, but she felt better for it. After a quick glance at the clock on the back wall, she realized she only had a few minutes left before her shift ended.

She'd been here way before the diner had opened for breakfast helping Enya make the muffins, pies, and cakes. The place had been busy from the moment the doors had opened at the new time of seven and she hadn't taken a break. Delta had shoved a full bowl of clam chowder into her hands and then pointed toward the door. "Go and eat. When you're done, you can go home."

"But I—"

The other woman hadn't let her finish speaking. She'd pointed toward the door again, and then signed, "You're dead on your feet,

Lilac. You've been working since four in the morning for the last month. Are you sure you're okay? You're really pale."

"I'm always pale." Lilac smiled.

"I know, but you're paler than normal."

"I'm fine."

Delta looked at her skeptically but didn't say anything. Lilac didn't want to get into the story in regard to her skin or eye coloring, or that she was having nightmares. There was no way she was going to put a damper on her new friend's happiness.

"Go eat." Delta pointed toward the door again. "When you're done, go home and get some rest."

"Aye, aye, captain." Lilac grinned and mock saluted her friend and then headed out.

"Do you want more coffee?" Enya's question brought Lilac back to the present.

"No, thanks." She picked up her bowl and cup and carried them back to the kitchen. After rinsing the dishes and putting in the dishwasher she waved to Delta, gathered her things from the cupboard in the storage room and walked down the hall toward the diner and the exit.

She'd just reached the end of the serving counter when she glanced toward the door. Her heart missed a beat and then slammed painfully against her sternum. Sweat sheened over her skin, and yet she shivered with cold. The trembling fear started in the pit of her stomach and rippled out through her whole body until she was sure the quaking was visible to anyone who cared to look. Lilac wanted to step backward, away from the diner's glass front and door, but she wasn't sure her legs would remain under her. Her knees felt as if they would buckle beneath her at any moment.

"Are you all right, ma'am?"

The question came from a long way away, and while she nodded, she wasn't sure she'd ever be all right again.

"Whoa." Someone gripped her elbow. "Why don't you come and sit down before you fall."

Lilac didn't even realize she was panting until she turned her head to look at whoever was holding on to her arm. She was about to tell them to let her go, but the words got caught in her throat when she looked up, and up, and up some more. Standing to her right was one of the men she'd seen watching her earlier, and while he was as handsome as sin, she didn't know him from Adam.

"I'm fine." She jerked her arm from his grip and had to bite the inside of her cheek when she hit her elbow on the corner of the counter. Tingles and numbness raced up her arm after hitting her funny bone and nerve hard enough to leave a bruise, but she ignored the discomfort and took a half step back.

"You don't look fine, Lilac."

She shifted her gaze to the man she hadn't seen standing beside the one who'd been holding her and forced a smile when she realized it was the sheriff who'd spoken.

"I'm okay, sheriff."

Luke shook his head, skirted around the handsome guy until he was standing in front of her, and narrowed his gaze. "Don't lie to me, Lilac. You look as if you've just seen a ghost."

She licked her suddenly dry lips and wondered if she should tell the sheriff about who she'd thought she'd seen. She shook her head. Going to the law hadn't helped her all those years ago, and because of that, she had trust issues. Yet Luke, Damon, and his deputies weren't like the sheriff in Bemidji. She'd seen them searching and helping others with her own eyes. Damon had been the one to stay with Enya after she'd been knocked unconscious when that crazy man had kidnapped Delta. He'd even ridden in the back of the ambulance to the new hospital that had been built on the far west side of town with her.

Luke nudged her chin up with a gentle finger beneath her chin, lifting her gaze to his. His expression was stern and earnest, and she realized he wasn't going to let her get away from him without telling him what he wanted to know.

She glanced at the other man, and heat crept into her cheeks when she found him staring at her intently. Heat shimmered in her middle and slowly spread outward, causing private places to react, and that scared her more than maybe seeing the cult leader's son.

Lilac had seen too many things to want to have this kind of reaction to any man, and yet her body had made the same response when she turned to see who was watching her earlier. Not one but the three identical men caused her dormant libido to perk up with interest, and that downright terrified her.

"Lilac?"

She hadn't noticed she'd zoned out until Luke called her name. She returned her gaze to his and nodded before turning toward the hallway and the diner office.

Her heart felt as if it was beating a hundred miles a minute and her breathing was shallow, but if she wanted to feel safe again, she needed to tell Luke what she was so scared of. Maybe he, Damon, and his deputies would be able to get the law to raid that cult and save the other young girls and women from a horrific fate. She'd been lucky to escape when she had. If she hadn't…she didn't want to think of where she would be.

None of that mattered anymore. She was free and she planned to stay that way.

Lilac entered the office and gasped when she saw that not only had Luke followed her, but so had Damon and three identical handsome men.

She frowned and crossed her arms beneath her breasts. "What are they doing here?"

"This is Wilder, Cree, and Nash Sheffield. I've just recruited them as new deputies. They start their shifts on Monday," Luke explained.

"But they aren't working yet, so they don't need to be here, do they," she stated firmly.

Luke glanced at Damon and then the Sheffield men before returning his gaze to hers. "Actually, they do."

"Why would—"

Luke interrupted. "You didn't let me finish, honey. Why don't you sit down? Do you want some water or something else to drink?"

Lilac shook her head. To an outsider, Luke's questions would have sounded patronizing, but she knew otherwise. He, Damon, and the deputies were all very caring people. The jury was still out on the Sheffield men.

"No, thanks. I'm fine." With a sigh of resignation, she glanced about the room trying to decide where to sit. She didn't want to sit on the sofa just in case one of the men in the room decided to sit next to her. Lilac kept away from the opposite sex as much as possible. The only time she was near a man was when she was serving in the diner, and she intended to keep it that way.

Decision made, she hurried over to the desk and chair behind it, taking deep breaths and hoping she didn't hyperventilate or break down while she explained her fear.

Once she was seated, Luke and Damon grabbed chairs and moved them closer to the desk before sitting down. She glanced over at the Sheffield men from under her lowered lashes to see they were standing against the wall and closed office door. She quickly looked away when her cheeks began to flush at being caught gazing at them. All three of them were leaning with their arms crossed, watching her avidly. It didn't help that they were all muscular with bulging biceps that drew her attention.

She drew another deep breath and locked gazes with Luke. It was safe to look at him and Damon since they were both married and in loving relationships. Plus, she wasn't attracted to them even though they were both handsome. "You didn't tell me why they're here." She pointed toward the men against the wall without looking at them.

"It just so happens that Wilder, Cree, and Nash have leased the house next door to your cottage."

No. No. No. Please no.

Lilac tried and hoped she kept her expression blank. She didn't want these men to realize she was horrified over that tidbit of information. "So what?" she asked with no intonation in her voice.

"So, if you're in trouble, they're in the perfect position to keep you safe." Damon leaned forward with his elbows resting on his knees.

"I'm not in trouble," Lilac hedged.

"Lilac, I do a background check on everyone coming into this town," Luke explained.

Lilac shrugged. She had nothing to hide. She'd never had a run-in with the law, and since she didn't own a car, she'd never had a speeding or parking fine. She realized something was wrong when Luke's gaze didn't waver. "And?"

"And on paper, honey, you don't exist."

"What?" she asked hoarsely and shook her head. "That's not possible. Of course, I exist. I'm sitting right in front of you."

"No, Lilac, you don't," Luke said in a gentle voice. "There isn't a record of Lilac Primrose ever being born."

"That's not possible," she whispered and tried to gasp air into her burning lungs. There was a loud roaring in her ears and her heart was beating so fast, it was hurting. Perspiration formed under her arms and trickled down between her breasts, and her stomach roiled with nausea.

She didn't even notice she was swaying in her seat until she blinked and the desk seemed to move before her very eyes. She swallowed the gorge rising in her throat, but when saliva pooled in her mouth she knew she was going to be sick.

Lilac shoved from her chair and stumbled toward the door. The three Sheffield men straightened, but the one who'd been leaning against the wood entrance didn't step aside. She saw a hand reaching toward her but shook her head as she sidestepped. "Move," was the only word she managed to get out before she covered her mouth.

One of the men opened the door for her, and Lilac bolted to the restroom. She only just made it into the cubicle and onto her knees before she lost the lunch she'd eaten not so very long ago. She didn't even have time to close and lock the door to the toilet behind her.

She heaved and heaved until there was nothing left to come up, but the spasming muscles wouldn't stop. Tears streamed from her eyes and down her face as she wretched over and over. Finally, after what seemed like forever, the involuntary contractions ceased.

After wiping her face with the back of her hands, she pushed to her feet, flushed the toilet and ignoring the shakiness in her legs, turned toward the sink, and turned the water on. She cupped the water in her hands, brought it to her mouth and rinsed the acidic taste away, and then splashed water onto her face.

Lilac couldn't help but stare at herself in the mirror above the sink. The face peering back at her was familiar, and yet she had no idea who she was.

Had the people in the cult changed her name after they'd kidnapped her from her home?

She'd been so young, not even five and while she'd tried to remember if she had parents, the memories wouldn't come. The only thing she could remember was that sweet floral scent. It had taken her years to realize the perfume that had haunted her childhood dreams was lavender, but those dreams had been quickly overridden with terrifying nightmares.

Those nightmares still plagued her today, and she had a feeling they would for the rest of her life.

Sometimes Lilac wondered if she'd ever be normal.

Chapter Three

"Fuck!" Wilder shoved his fingers through his hair and began to pace. He stopped and turned to face Luke. "Do you know who she is?"

Luke shook his head. "No, and from the shocked expression on her face, Lilac doesn't either. Shit! I can't believe I fucking screwed up."

"You couldn't have known, Luke," Damon said. "We thought that maybe she was in witness protection."

"So what the fuck is going on?" Cree asked.

"We don't know," Luke answered.

"Whatever it is, Lilac is terrified." Nash stuck his head out the door and peered up the hallway. "She's been in the restroom a while. Do you think we should go and see if she's all right? Or maybe send one of the other women in to check on her?"

"I'll get Enya," Damon replied just before he hurried from the room.

"There's something really strange going on here." Wilder scrubbed a hand over his face. "I don't like this, at all."

"I don't either, but we can't go jumping to conclusions, Wilder," Luke said. "We're going to need all the facts before we start trying to come up with scenarios."

Wilder nodded. He knew Luke was right, and though he tried he couldn't dislodge the knot of dread pitted in his gut. The hair in the back of his neck was standing on end, and that always meant trouble. His inbuilt radar or intuition had saved his neck a time or two while fighting in the Marines, and he'd learned to never discount his inner alarm. He ignored Damon when he returned to the office, too worried about Lilac to acknowledge the other man right now.

He glanced toward the door when he caught movement from the corner of his eye and was relieved to see Lilac and Enya near the entrance. Enya whispered something to Lilac and she nodded.

Lilac entered the room with her gaze lowered toward the floor, and while she was still very pale, she looked better than she had before she'd rushed out.

"Are you okay, Lilac?" Luke asked as he and Damon took their seats after she'd sat in the chair behind the desk again.

"Yeah, I'm okay."

"Are you all right if we ask you a few questions?" Damon asked gently.

Wilder glanced at Nash and pointed toward the door. Nash closed the office door and then leaned back against it. Cree hadn't moved from his post near the wall beside the door, but Wilder knew his identical brother as well as he knew himself. Cree was as tense as a bowstring. The muscles in his upper arms were twitching as were his pecs, and he kept clenching and unclenching his hands.

Cree was just as uptight as he and Nash were. His brother was grinding his teeth, causing the muscles on either side of his jaw to flex.

Wilder glanced back toward Lilac when she swallowed audibly, and she nodded.

"Do you know what your real name is?" Damon asked.

When Wilder saw the moisture welling in Lilac's eyes, he wanted to hurry around the desk, scoop her up into his arms, and hold her, but he forced himself to remain where he was. Lilac didn't know him or his brothers, but if he had the chance to change that, he would take advantage. It didn't matter that he didn't know her, he knew she was the right woman for him and his brothers. He just hoped that whatever was going on didn't make it harder for them to woo her.

"I thought Lilac Primrose was my real name."

Wilder drew a deep breath and held it as anger surged through his body. He wasn't angry at Lilac but angry on her behalf. She looked so small and fragile sitting in that office chair. She was as white as milk and her shoulders were slumped in defeat. His heart went out to her, and again the urge to hold her and comfort her nearly overrode all his good intentions to remain where he was.

"Can you tell me about your parents?" Luke asked.

She shook her head and more tears welled. Even though she blinked rapidly as if trying to keep from crying, the moisture brimmed before spilling down her cheeks. "I don't know who my parents are," she wailed softly. "I've spent the last ten years searching, but I haven't been able to find them."

Wilder couldn't take it another moment. He moved around behind the desk and squatted down next to Lilac, palming both of her cheeks. He swiped the tears from her face with his thumbs, and though he wanted to kiss her on the lips, he settled for leaning in and kissing her on the forehead. "It's going to be okay, love."

She shook her head. "How can it? I don't know who I am."

Pain gripped his heart at the fear and despondency he saw her in unusual gorgeous, violet eyes. And in the next instant she threw herself at him, her arms looped around his neck and she sobbed into his neck. Wilder wrapped his arms around her waist, stood, taking her with him, and then sat in the office chair with Lilac on his lap. His heart broke all over again when he felt her shaking as she cried but not once did she make a sound. Who the hell had hurt her so badly? He knew she'd been hurt. No one cried the way she did, so hard without making any noise.

What the hell had happened to Lilac Primrose?

* * * *

Cree shoved away from the wall and hurried over to stand behind Wilder and Lilac. He glanced over at Nash when he came to stand next to him. Without saying a word to each other, they placed their hands on her shoulders and gave a gentle squeeze, letting her know that they were here for her just as Wilder was.

Cree shifted his gaze to Luke and Damon. Anger surged through his blood again when he saw the concern on the sheriffs' faces. How could Lilac not know who her parents were? Had she been a ward of the state? Had she grown up in foster care?

What the fuck is going on?

Lilac's shaking slowed to an occasional shudder, and Cree knew her tears were slowing. He hated seeing her so upset and vulnerable, and vowed then and there to do everything he could to help her out. He sifted his free hand through his short-cropped hair and concentrated on keeping his breathing deep and regular. If he let his emotions get control, he could end up frightening Lilac and that was something he never, ever wanted to do.

She shuddered under his other hand, and after drawing in a deep ragged breath she sat up a little straighter, wiped her cheeks with the back of her hands, and sniffed.

Nash reached for the box of tissues sitting on the desk and snagged a couple before pushing them into Lilac's hand.

"Thanks," she rasped before blotting her cheeks and then blowing her nose.

"Do you want something to drink, honey?" Cree asked, squeezing her shoulder again.

"Water, please."

"I'll get it," Damon said as he stood and hurried out. He came back a few moments later with an armful of water bottles and handed them around after giving Lilac hers first.

Cree slugged down half the bottle while watching Wilder caress his hand up and down Lilac's back as she sipped at the water.

"Are you okay, baby?" Nash asked with concern.

"I'm good. Sorry, I didn't mean to fall apart." Lilac glanced over her shoulder at Cree, then looked at Nash, Wilder, and the sheriffs.

"Don't apologize, Lilac," Wilder stroked his hand up her back. "You've just had a huge shock."

Lilac laughed a little hysterically and ended up choking and spluttering since she'd just taken a sip of water. Wilder patted her on the back until she was breathing normally once again.

"Where did you grow up, Lilac?" Damon asked.

"I can't remember the first few years of my life, since I was too young, but I grew up in Werner, Minnesota, from the age of four or five years old, until I was fifteen."

"Where did you go once you were fifteen?" Wilder asked.

"I headed to New York City. I didn't have much cash and it took me twelve months of working and traveling to reach my final destination."

"You were on your own? Traveling by yourself when you were only fifteen?" Cree asked incredulously.

"Yes."

"What—" Nash didn't get to finish his question because Luke cut him off.

"You need to tell us everything you can remember, Lilac. If we're going to figure out who you are and find your family, you need to talk to us."

Cree shifted to the side so he could see her face. She was tense and wringing her hands in her lap, but she was also nodding. He glanced about the room and spotted another couple of chairs near the small sofa and the far wall. He nodded to Nash to go get them. His brother looked reluctant to move away from Lilac but didn't argue. Cree tensed when Lilac slid to her feet and paced away from Wilder and the desk. When she got close to the door, Cree's stomach dropped. He was worried she was about to take off, but when she leaned against the entrance with her back to the door and her arms crossed beneath her breasts, he exhaled softly.

Luke held up his cell phone. "Do you mind if I record all of this?"

Lilac shook her head, drew in a deep breath, and then started talking. "I lived with a group of people just outside of Werner in Minnesota as I said. There were only a few children but there were a lot of adults. We were home schooled and were never allowed off the property. I didn't know that wasn't how other kids grew up, not until I was about twelve years old."

"What changed to make you realize you were living a different life?" Damon asked.

"I was a bit of a rebel." Lilac tried to smile, but it came out more like a grimace. "I was bored and lonely. The two other girls I spent most of my time with hadn't finished their chores, but I had, so I went for a walk. The ten or so acres of land had high fences all the way around and there was barbed wire on the top. We were told that it was to keep us safe from intruders, from evil, but they lied." Lilac paused to take another sip of water. "It was to keep us in and from others seeing in.

"I was feeling trapped and lonely and decided to see what was so scary on the other side of the fence. I climbed a mountain maple tree that was close to the fence. The things I saw. There were kids in buses and cars whizzing by. At first it was frightening but that fear quickly turned to excitement. I don't know how long I was up in that tree staring out at the world with fascination, but it must have been a long time." Lilac lowered her gaze to the floor.

"They came looking for me. The leader sent out the teenage boys to search for me, and his son, Virgil, found me. That little shit was as nice as pie to me until I was back on the ground. The moment my feet touched down he grabbed my arm and slapped me across the face. I was so shocked I didn't even cry out."

Cree's knuckles cracked when he clenched his fists. "How old was he?"

"Seventeen."

"That motherfucking son of a bitch," Nash snarled.

"Fuck!" Wilder growled.

Lilac continued on as if there hadn't been any outbursts. "He dragged me back to the main house and into his father's den. His father just stared at me without showing any emotion for a good long while, and then he smiled. There was so much evil in his cold hazel eyes I actually took a step back, but the asshole's son was behind me and shoved me forward. He pushed me so hard I fell onto my hands and knees, and just as I was about to get up, his father stood. 'Stay where you are you little bitch,' the leader yelled.

"But I got to my feet and glared at him as he walked around the desk. He stood in front of me only inches away and then reached out and gripped my hair, yanking my head back until my neck hurt and I was scared he was going to snap it."

Cree blinked through the haze of red rage coloring his vision. He wanted to demand that Lilac give him the name of the man and son who'd hurt her so he could hunt them down and rip them apart with his bare hands, but he kept silent. He was scared if he opened his mouth he'd roar with rage and scare off the one woman who was meant to be his and his brothers'. He inhaled deeply and released the breath slowly as he tried to quell his ire.

He glanced at his brothers and the sheriffs and from the heat in their eyes, they were just as furious as he was.

"He told me that if I said anything about what I'd seen he would beat me within an inch of my life." When she lifted her gaze and Cree saw the fear in her eyes, he took a step toward her. She held up her hand and shook her head. "I need to finish this."

Cree's heart filled with pride. He was proud of Lilac's strength and bravery, and in that moment, he fell a little in love with her. When she started speaking again, he pushed his emotions aside and drew on his military training. No matter what happened between Lilac, him, and his brothers, he was going to find the bastard's who'd hurt their woman and take them down.

"From that moment on Virgil, the son, and his cronies became my shadow. The only time I was ever left alone was when I went to the bathroom and bed. They must have told the girls I shared a room with that I'd done something terrible because the only time they ever spoke to me was when we were doing chores together and they only ever talked about what we were doing. I was surrounded by people, but I was isolated from everybody."

"What's the father's name?" Damon asked angrily. "Can you show us on a map where this place was?"

"I haven't finished," Lilac said sadly.

Cree wasn't sure how much more he could take. He couldn't believe a child had grown up in such isolation under such fear and control. He was so fucking angry he was shaking.

"The day I turned fifteen was a day I will never forget. My shadows and the rest of the men were called into the leader's office for a meeting. The other girls and I were in the vegetable garden with the women pulling weeds and tending to the few farm animals we had. It was a hot day and I was thirsty after spending hours under the hot summer sun. Everyone was sweating, so I went back inside to get jugs of water and glasses to take back outside."

Nash was panting as if he was about to explode, and although Wilder had his arms crossed, he was gripping his biceps so hard he was leaving marks in his flesh. Cree wondered if his face was as red as it felt. He was so fucking angry he felt as if his face was on fire.

"I heard the men arguing in the den. I knew I shouldn't go down that hall and listen in, but when I heard my name mentioned I had to know what they were talking about. I snuck down the hall and stopped just beside the slightly open door and covered my mouth with my hand so they didn't hear me breathing." Lilac paused as a shudder raced through her body, causing her to shake. She tightened her arms around her ribs and bent over slightly as if she was in pain, and she was. Cree could see the emotional stress and horror on her face even though she wasn't even looking at him. The whole time she'd been talking, she'd been speaking in monotone as if she was far removed from the situation as possible, but he knew that wasn't the case. Yes, she'd distanced herself so she could tell her story, but only so she wouldn't break apart. Her lips were in a tight line and her eyes had narrowed to a squint as if she had a headache. After all that crying before and now relieving these horrid years of her childhood, she probably had the headache from hell.

"'You're not giving her to Mills,' Virgil shouted at his father. 'You let him bed Fleur and Warren was allowed to deflower Rose. If anyone's going to fuck that slut on her sixteenth birthday, it's going to be me.' That was the moment I knew I had to escape. I was only two months away from turning sixteen. There was no way I was staying just so he could..." Lilac shook her head and slid down the door until her ass hit the floor. She doubled over clutching her stomach as she sobbed.

Cree rushed over to her, knelt at her feet, and reached for her, but he hesitated over touching her. Yes, he was attracted to her and wanted to have a relationship with her, but right now, he wanted to comfort her more. He'd never thought about comforting a woman and wasn't sure how to go about it, but her pain was beating at him and he couldn't let her think she was in this alone. He and his brothers would protect her even if it meant using their bodies to shield her from a bullet. She already meant that much to him.

Lilac rubbed the tears from her eyes and face, drew a deep breath, and lifted her gaze. She jerked when she saw Cree so close to her, but when she locked gazes with his, the tension seemed to drain right out of her.

"You don't have to continue if you don't want to, honey." Cree held his hand out to her. "Let me help you up from the floor. Do you want to sit on the sofa?"

Lilac sucked in a shuddering breath and nodded as she placed her hand into his. Her hand was so small and pale compared to his large, bronzed appendage, he was worried about hurting her. She was shaking, but as soon as he enveloped her hand into his, she gripped him hard, as if he was the only lifeline she had when her world had turned upside down.

Cree was careful of his strength when he clasped her upper arm with his other hand and helped her to her feet. He hooked his arm around her waist when she swayed and then guided her over to the sofa. She sighed wearily when she sank into the cushion, and Cree sat right beside her, keeping her hand clasped with his. Luke and Damon stood, turned their chairs around until they were facing the sofa, and sat down again. Wilder walked toward the sofa slowly and perched on the arm. Nash moved sit on the floor near Lilac's feet, but he didn't sit too close in case she felt hemmed in.

"How did you escape Lilac?" Luke asked in a quiet, gentle voice.

"I'd been planning on leaving for a while, but when I heard them talking about letting Virgil rape me, I knew I had to leave as soon as possible. There was money stored in a tin in the kitchen for supplies. The women used it every week to buy things we needed. They went once a week, every Wednesday morning. Since it was Wednesday afternoon and they'd already bought what was needed, there was no reason for them to look in the tin again. I went back to the kitchen and took what cash was left and then crept to my bedroom where I'd been hiding nonperishable food under a loose floorboard. I wrapped the money and food up a shirt and shoved it under my pillow. For the rest of the day I went about my chores as if nothing had changed."

She gazed into Cree's eyes. "I was so scared I would give myself away. I was on tenterhooks the rest of the afternoon and night, but no one looked at me any differently.

"I went through the motions of getting ready for bed and for the first time in my life I was grateful for the big, long nightgowns we'd been given to wear. I kept my clothes on under the gown and got into bed and pretended to sleep. The time passed so quickly and yet it seemed to drag by.

"Finally, I got up, removed the gown, put my hooded sweatshirt on, grabbed the shirt with the food and money, and snuck out."

"How did you get over the barbed wire?" Nash's voice was hoarse.

"I climbed that tree, walked along a thick branch, and jumped."

"Shit. You could have been hurt, sweetness." Wilder rubbed at the back of his neck.

"Better that than what I was leaving behind," Lilac snapped.

"You're right. I wasn't...I didn't...I'm sorry." Wilder squeezed Lilac's shoulder.

"What did you do then?" Luke asked.

"I walked from just outside of Werner to Bemidji. It shouldn't have taken as long as it did, but I was so scared of getting caught and being dragged back there. Every time I heard a car coming I hid and waited for it to pass before I resumed walking again. It took me five hours, and when I got to the bus line building I had to wait another couple of hours for the terminal to open. As soon as I could, I got onto the first bus leaving town and never looked back."

"Thank fuck you got away, baby." Nash smoothed a hand up and down her trouser covered shin.

Lilac nodded, her face pale and her expression grim.

Cree vowed then and there that no one was ever going to hurt Lilac Primrose again. Not on his and his brother's watch. Even if it was the last thing he ever did, they would protect her with their lives.

* * * *

Nash was so angry he wanted to hit something or someone. Preferably the assholes that had kept Lilac and the other girls locked away behind a high fence and barbed wire. If he ever found those fuckers, he wouldn't lose any sleep over scoping them through his sniper rifle and pulling the trigger.

"Where did you go?" Cree asked.

"I ended up in New York. The first few nights I stayed in a women's shelter, but when the counselor started urging me to talk to her to find out where I was from and who I was running from, I left."

"Why?" Luke asked. "Why didn't you go to the local sheriff's office?"

Nash tensed when she snorted and laughed a little hysterically. "The first thing I did was go to the Bemidji Sheriff's Department. After Virgil and his cohorts started shadowing me, I started writing everything down. The other girls thought I was keeping a journal and I guess in a way I was, but it was evidence. Evidence of the evil deeds those people did.

"I stood in the shadows under a tree and wrote them how I'd been virtually kept prisoner, locked away from society, and that they were planning and had condoned rape. The sheriff's office was closed, but I pushed the paper under the door." Lilac stared at Luke. "Nothing was done. I used local libraries to search the internet on any news regarding Werner and the surrounding county. The sheriff and his deputies didn't do anything."

The rage that crossed Luke's face was so fierce Nash wondered if he was going to explode. Luke glanced at Damon and nodded.

"No wonder you didn't trust anyone in authority," Damon stated. "Did you end up on the streets?"

Nash wanted to pound his fist into the floor. The thought of Lilac at the age of fifteen being on the streets with all the pimps, hookers, and drug dealers was so horrifying, it felt as if his blood was boiling and freezing at the same time.

"Not really," Lilac answered Damon.

"What do you mean, not really?" Cree asked.

Lilac sighed. "It took me twelve months to work my way across to New York. I was lucky enough that I had skills dealing with food since I had to cook for everyone along with the other two girls. I worked in diners and cafes helping chefs with food preparation, as well as waiting on customers and washing dishes."

"Where did you sleep?" Wilder asked before Nash could.

She glanced at each of them before lowering her eyes to the floor. "Bus terminals, subways, and the like. Sometimes I was lucky enough to room with one of the other staff."

"And after you left the shelter, where did you go?" Nash asked.

"I had enough money to enroll into school." She gnawed on her lips nervously.

Luke leaned forward in his seat. "And?"

"I did my homework in the school library until I was kicked out and then I'd sneak into the basement. I'd been able to pick up a sleeping bag at a secondhand shop. I set up a living space in the corner of the school basement. I was able to use the showers in the gym, and there was always food on hand since there was a large cafeteria." Lilac smiled.

Nash's breath caught in his lungs. Her violet eyes lightened and there was a sparkle in them. Her lips were a lush Cupid's bow, and when she licked them, he couldn't help wondering what they tasted like. They were a tempting light pink color, which had him thinking about other parts of her body. When he realized where his mind was going, he pushed the lascivious thoughts aside and brought his mind back on track.

"The school janitor caught me in the basement halfway through the second week. I thought I was in trouble and was so scared, but he was wonderful. He put me at ease and then led me across to the other side of the basement. There in the corner was a bunk bed and a rack with clothes hanging from it. He was elderly, and though he'd lost everything in the financial crash, he was happy enough.

"We struck up a friendship, and after a few weeks, I moved my bedding near his. He made me feel safe and I hadn't felt that way in a long, long time." Lilac shrugged nonchalantly.

Nash could see that the friendship had meant a lot to her. He would love to find the man and offer him a home. When he noticed tears pooling in Lilac's eyes, he held his breath.

"His name was Sam and he had no living relatives, no family, just like me. He died just before I graduated high school." Lilac sniffed and cleared her throat.

"I'm sorry, baby." Nash stroked down her shin.

"What did you do after high school?" Cree asked.

"I enrolled in culinary school on a scholarship and was lucky enough to be picked up by a renowned restaurant in New York City when I had my degree." Lilac shrugged again, but Nash knew she had to have worked hard in school to be picked up by a popular restaurant right out of college.

"How did you end up here, in Slick Rock?" Damon asked.

Lilac sucked in a noisy breath and shivered as if she was scared. Nash wanted to pull her into his arms and offer her comfort but he refrained. She didn't seem comfortable being the center of male attention. She'd tugged her hand out of Wilder's just after starting her story, and she'd shifted away from his brothers, making sure they weren't touching in any way. He hoped that eventually she would get used to having them around and even concede to having a relationship with them, but he wasn't sure she'd agree. Nash, Wilder, and Cree were going to have to be patient with Lilac.

"I was on my way to work my shift and saw the leader's son walking toward the restaurant. He hadn't seen me, so I ducked into another shop and watched him out the window. When he entered the restaurant, I knew he'd been searching for me."

Nash scrambled up onto his knees and gazed into her frightened eyes. "Is that why you were scared earlier? Did you see this asshole?"

"I can't be sure because it's been just over ten years, but I thought I saw someone who looked like it could be him."

"Were you being kept in a cult, Lilac?" Luke asked.

Lilac nodded slowly.

"Shit! Why the fuck didn't the sheriff in Bemidji do something?" Cree scowled.

"I don't know," Damon replied. "But you can bet your ass we're going to find out."

"We're going to need names, Lilac," Luke stated.

"I'll give them to you, but what can you do? You need proof, evidence that these people are doing something illegal. For all I know, they could have adopted me and the other girls." Lilac covered her face with her hands and then lowered them again. "I wanted to take them with me, but I couldn't trust them."

"You did the right thing, honey," Damon said.

"Did I? If I did then why do I feel so guilty? Those bastards were raping those girls and were intending on raping me."

"Do you know for sure it was rape?" Luke asked.

Nash stood when Lilac did and he was about to clasp her hand in his, but she moved around him and started pacing. "From what I overheard I'd have to say yes, but I'm not a hundred percent certain."

"How old were the boys?" Wilder asked.

"They were eighteen and nineteen. Rose and Fleur were older than me." Lilac frowned. "Rose was twelve months and Fleur was eighteen months older."

"They might have consented," Luke said.

Lilac glared at him. "And they might not have."

"I'll be looking into it, Lilac, don't think I won't. However, if those girls don't press charges, there's nothing we can do."

"What we need to do is find out who you are," Damon said.

"How are you going to do that?" Lilac asked.

Nash moved to stand in front of her and gazed into her amazingly gorgeous, unusual eyes. "We're going to search every missing person's database."

"You don't know if I'm missing." She frowned.

"We'll look at all the records of adopted children in the States," Cree said.

"How old are you, sweetness?" Wilder asked.

"If those people didn't lie about my birthdate, then I'm twenty-five. I'll be twenty-six on December 31."

"You're a New Year's Eve baby?" Nash asked.

"As far as I know." Lilac sighed and rubbed at her eyes.

"Give me the names, Lilac," Luke ordered in a firm voice.

She sighed. "The son's name is Virgil Kennedy. His friends are Grant Mills and Warren Gordon."

"And the father?" Damon asked.

"Messiah Kennedy."

"How many men were in this cult?" Luke asked.

"Fifteen including the teenage boys."

"How many women?" Damon asked.

"Five, not including Rose, Fleur, and myself."

She looked absolutely exhausted. Nash hoped she'd finished working for the day. Now that he knew she lived next door to him and his brothers, he was going to keep an eye on her.

If the guy from the cult was in Slick Rock, he and his brothers were going to make sure Lilac was safe.

No one was getting their hands on her if he could help it.

Chapter Four

"I want to go home." Lilac was so tired she could barely keep her eyes open. She was physically and emotionally exhausted. While she'd never told anyone what her life had been like growing up in a cult besides Sam, she was relieved she had. She felt lighter, as if the burden of those ten horrible years had lifted from her shoulders.

She'd been petrified of anyone in law enforcement for a long time, but after watching Luke, Damon, and the other deputies, she'd realized they were good, honest, hard-working men trying to keep the surrounding county safe.

"We can take you home," Wilder said as he stood.

She shook her head. "I usually walk."

"Baby, you're nearly asleep on your feet," Nash said. "According to the sheriff, we live right next door to you and we're going home anyway. Let us give you a ride."

Lilac wasn't sure how to react to the Sheffield men calling her by pet names, but she didn't want to get on their bad side by saying anything. For all she knew, they called all women sweet names.

"Okay. Thank you." The other men got to the feet, and they all headed toward the front of the diner and outside.

Lilac inhaled the clean country air deeply into her lungs and released it again on a weary sigh. She didn't even notice that she'd closed her eyes until someone clasped her elbow.

She met Cree's concerned gaze and tried to smile. She realized she'd failed miserably when he frowned down at her.

"Me or Damon will be in touch, Lilac. Go home and get some rest," Luke ordered.

Normally she would have been pissed off at being told what to do because she'd been on her own since she was young, but right now she was too tired to argue, so she just nodded.

"Come on, sweetness," Wilder said as he laced his fingers with her hand. He and Cree guided her down the street toward their vehicle.

Cree opened the back door to a late-model truck and lifted her up into the cab. She scooted across the seat and glanced around for Nash.

"Wait! I forgot my…bag."

Before she'd said the word "bag," Nash had exited the diner clutching her purse. He held it up and grinned as he hurried toward the truck. Wilder got into the driver's seat, and Nash got into the front passenger seat. He turned to gaze at her over his shoulder. "I figured you'd need your purse so you could get into your house."

Lilac nodded. "Thank you."

Nash winked and smiled. "You're welcome, baby."

Cree shifted in the seat beside her gaining her attention. "Are you living in the small white house with the blue trim?"

"Yes."

"That's a pretty place," Wilder said as he started the truck, checked the mirrors and turned so he could back out of the parking space.

"I like it."

"We're leasing the house on the left of yours," Cree said.

"That's nice," Lilac replied tiredly and then covered her mouth when she yawned.

She tried to keep her eyes open, but getting up at 4:00 a.m. every morning for weeks on end and dealing with broken sleep because of her nightmares had finally caught up with her. Lilac rested her head back against the seat and closed her eyes.

She was asleep in seconds.

* * * *

"She's asleep." Cree met Wilder's gaze in the rearview mirror.

"She's exhausted," Nash said over his shoulder.

"Yeah," Wilder agreed.

"What do we do when we get home?" Cree asked.

"What do you mean?" Nash frowned.

"Do you think she'd be upset if we went through her purse looking for her house keys, or should we just carry her into our place?" Cree combed his fingers through his hair.

"We'll wait and see," Wilder said. "She might wake up when we stop the truck."

"How do you think Lilac ended up living in a cult?" Nash asked.

"Hell if I know," Cree replied.

"The only way to know for sure is if Lilac remembers, but she said herself, she couldn't remember things because she'd been too young." Wilder checked his mirrors and indicated before turning the corner.

"I wonder if she'd been willing to be hypnotized?" Nash mused.

"Hey, that's not a bad idea," Cree said.

"Hold on, you two." Wilder slowed the truck and turned onto their street. "You can't just go giving Lilac orders. As she said earlier, she's been looking after herself since she was fucking fifteen years old."

"I wasn't going to fucking order her to do anything, Wilder. You should know me better than that," Nash snarled.

Wilder sighed. "Yeah, I do. Sorry. It's just that…" He shook his head as he turned onto their driveway and finally stopped the truck in front of the house.

"We're all in stormy waters," Cree said. "None of us have ever been in a short-term relationship, let alone vying for a long-term one."

"I want her so bad." Wilder shut the engine off and opened the door. He turned to stare at Lilac's beautiful face. "She's everything."

"She is, but we need to give her time to get to know us." Cree reached over and clapped Wilder on the shoulder. "I think she trusts us as well as Luke and Damon."

"How the hell could you know that?" Wilder asked.

"I don't think she's ever told anyone about where she grew up." Cree smiled as his gaze wandered over Lilac's face.

"I think she told that janitor, Sam," Nash said. "I wish like hell he was still alive. I would have gone to New York and brought him back to live with us."

"We all would have, Nash."

"So what do we do now?" Cree asked.

"Women are strange about their purses. I think we should bring her inside and let her sleep in the spare room," Wilder suggested.

"I have to agree." Nash nodded.

"Me, too," Cree said.

"Then let's go get our woman comfortable." Nash got out of the truck.

Cree gently lifted Lilac into his arms and maneuvered them both out of the back seat. He kept his gait slow and fluid so he didn't end up waking Lilac as he carried her inside.

He hoped that she would spend more and more time with him and his brothers, but he wasn't about to hold his breath.

Lilac had every right to be wary of the opposite sex after what she'd had to deal with growing up, but he had a feeling that she'd only touched on some of the things she'd dealt with while living at the cult. Although he wanted to know everything about her, he wasn't sure he'd be able to contain his anger when and if she told them more.

* * * *

Lilac cringed when she heard laughter outside her bedroom door. She pulled the blankets up over her head and held her breath, praying they would go away, but she knew they wouldn't.

Her heart stopped beating in her chest and then slammed painfully against her ribs, and though she tried to regulate her breathing, she still ended up panting breathlessly. The doorknob rattled and the hinges squeaked as the door was pushed open.

She peeked from under to blanket toward the other two single beds and quickly closed her eyes when she saw they were empty. She had no idea where Rose and Fleur were, but right now she wished they were in their own beds. Maybe if they had been, he wouldn't have come into her room.

The door nicked shut and she held her breath again, when she heard footsteps coming toward her. She didn't need to look to know who was there. He was always watching her with lust in his eyes, and when no one was watching he'd grab at his crotch lewdly.

She kept her lids lowered but watched him from beneath her lashes. When he was close enough, he reached out and grabbed the bed covers. Lilac screamed as she rolled to her feet and faced the bastard. He didn't seem at all fazed by her angry glare. The asshole actually smiled at her.

"Get out."

"No. You're sixteen today, Lilac. It's time you learned what a woman's for."

"You aren't going to touch me, you sick bastard."

"Is that right?" Virgil took a step closer, and while she wanted to step back, she had nowhere to go. "You're wasting both of our time and energy by fighting me, Lilac. I'll have what I want in the end."

That's what you think, you prick.

It didn't matter that she'd grown up isolated and away from society. She'd read a lot of books and knew how to defend herself. Putting what she'd learned academically into practice was another thing. Thankfully, the bedside lamp was on and she could see Virgil's face. She kept her gaze on his and waited for his next move. She breathed deeply and kept her muscles loose, and when he reached for her, she grabbed his wrist, twisted his arm as she spun into him, and flipped him over her hip.

He crashed into the bedside table, sending the lamp crashing to the floor. Lilac didn't wait to see if she'd hurt him or watch him get to his feet if she hadn't. She ran for the bedroom door and then down the hallway heading for the front door.

And then the nightmare changed.

Lilac was no longer the sixteen-year-old girl trying to fight off the boy intent on raping her.

She was standing in a strangely familiar room, and when she looked down she noticed the blanket covered in teddy bears. Her heart was racing and she wanted to scream for her mommy, but she was too scared to call for her.

She didn't even notice she was lying on her belly, hiding under the coffee table until she tried to sit up and hit her head. She wanted to cry when she hurt herself, but she put her clenched fist in her mouth and bit down. She couldn't make a noise or the bad men would see her.

Her mommy was crying on the floor, and the bad men were hitting and kicking her. She pulled her fist from her mouth and was just about to crawl over to her mother, but Mommy shook her head.

Tears rolled down her face as she watched the bad men hurt her mommy over and over again. Just before her mommy closed her eyes, she said, "I love you, Violet."

The big man with the star on his chest kicked her mom one more time and then turned toward her. Violet curled into a small ball and hoped the man wouldn't see her. The coffee table was lifted from over her and then crashed into the wall when the man with the star on his chest threw it.

Violet screamed and screamed when he grabbed her arm and lifted her from the floor.

"Shut up, you little bitch." Star Man slapped her face, stunning her into silence.

Violet kept her eyes on her mommy as Star Man carried her toward the door and out of the house.

* * * *

Wilder was on his feet with gun in hand before he blinked the sleep from his eyes. He was instantly alert even though his vision took a few seconds to clear. He opened his bedroom door a crack and peered out into the hall. When he didn't see anyone, he stepped out of his room and wasn't surprised to see Cree and Nash with their weapons at the ready.

"Cree check the kitchen and living room," Wilder whispered his order.

Cree nodded and walked silently down the hall.

"Nash search the laundry and back entrance."

Nash was already moving before Wilder had finished giving his command.

Wilder stood in the hallway with his head canted as he listened intently. Something wasn't right. Something out of the ordinary had woken him and his brothers. He glanced into his brothers' bedrooms, his gaze zeroing in on the windows, but they were still closed.

His barefoot didn't make any sound as he moved toward the spare bedroom where they'd left Lilac sleeping. Wilder was about to press his ear to the door but clasped the door handle instead when he heard a noise coming from her room.

With his gun ready, the safety off, he opened the door and scanned quickly. There was no one lurking about in the shadows and the adjoining bathroom door was still closed. He crept across the room, and after checking to make sure the en-suite was clear he turned to look at Lilac.

What he saw broke his fucking heart. She was curled up in a tight ball, tears streaming down her cheeks, and she was rocking in her sleep. What worried him most was the way she was sucking her thumb. He didn't give a shit if that was a quirk she'd had left over from childhood, but he didn't think it was.

Wilder's instincts were going crazy. Only a very small child sucked their thumb. He moved closer to Lilac and sat on the edge of the bed. His first instinct was to lift her into his lap and wrap his arms around her, but he didn't want to scare her.

"All clear," Nash said as he entered the room.

"Nothing," Cree whispered as he came in behind Nash.

"Lilac, wake up, sweetness. You're having a bad dream."

"Mommy, help me!" Lilac screamed after she pulled her thumb from her mouth and bolted upright.

"Fuck!" Cree groaned.

"Geezus." Nash sighed.

Wilder shifted onto his knees on the mattress and cupped Lilac's face between his hands. "You're safe, Lilac. We won't let anyone hurt you, sweetness. Come on, now. Wake up."

She took a shuddering breath and blinked. Wilder knew she was finally out of her nightmare when the haze receded from her gorgeous violet eyes.

"I remembered," she sobbed and then threw herself against him.

Wilder swallowed around the emotion constricting his throat as he wrapped his arms around her small body and hugged her tight. He shifted from his knees, back onto his ass at the edge of the mattress, and rocked back and forth, hoping the motion would calm her down. She was crying so hard her body was shaking and jerking, but what cut him up even more was that she didn't make a sound, again.

"It's okay, sweetness. I've got you." Wilder glanced at his brothers and then nodded toward the pistol he'd left on the bedside table. He didn't want Lilac seeing his gun and getting upset.

Cree hurried over, picked up Wilder's gun, and after making sure the safety was on, left with Nash to put them away.

When Wilder felt Lilac slump against him and take a ragged breath, he knew she'd stopped crying. "I'm sorry. All I ever seem to do around you and your brothers is cry."

"You have every reason to shed a few tears, sweetness."

Lilac shifted on his thighs, wiped the tears from her face, and then gazed about the room. "Where am I?"

"You're in our home, Lilac. You fell asleep in the truck, and since we didn't want to be rude by going through your purse and into your house, we brought you to our spare room."

"Thanks." She pushed at his arms, and with a sigh of reluctance Wilder let her go. She scrambled from his lap and glanced at him before quickly looking away. He bit back a grin when he saw the blush suffusing her cheeks. Their Lilac was shy. He was glad that he'd decided to sleep in his boxers instead of in the nude like he usually did.

"Are you all right, Lilac?" Cree asked as he leaned against the door frame.

"Yes," she whispered.

Nash shoved Cree out of his way and walked toward Lilac. He halted when she backed up. "I'd never hurt you, baby. Don't be scared of me or my brothers."

"What did you mean you remembered?" Wilder asked as he rose.

"It doesn't matter," Lilac said as she glanced toward the door.

"Of course it fucking matters," Wilder said. "Anything to do with you matters, sweetness."

"I need to go home."

Wilder wasn't about to let her leave after dropping that statement, and he didn't like the pain he could see in those beautiful eyes.

"What you need to do is talk to us, Lilac. As of Monday, we are going to be deputies. If you have more information so we can find out who you are, then you have to tell us."

"I already know who I am," she shouted. "My mother is dead."

Wilder grabbed hold of her waist when she started to collapse. He swept her up into his arms and held her tight against his chest. This time when she cried she sobbed loudly. The deep gut-wrenching sounds brought tears to his own eyes, and he had to clench his jaw to stave them off. When he glanced at Cree and Nash, he saw his brothers were hurting just as much as he was, but he knew it couldn't be as bad as the pain Lilac was feeling.

He wanted to roar out his rage, but he swallowed around the lump in his throat instead and sank back down to sit on the mattress. Lilac wrapped her arm around his neck and buried her face against his neck. Her tears flowed fast plopping onto his bare shoulder before rolling down his back and chest. She gasped in a breath and cried even harder. Although he was glad she was finally crying like she should, he was worried she was going to make herself sick. He caressed a hand up and down her back trying to soothe her pain, and while he wanted to say something to comfort her, he knew nothing he said would ease the turmoil she was in.

After what seemed like forever, her tears slowed until she was hiccupping spasmodically and then she sighed with exhaustion.

"My name isn't Lilac Primrose. It's Violet Evans."

"Are you sure, baby?" Nash asked as he sat on the bed beside them.

"Yes. I'm positive."

"Thank you for telling us, sweetness." Wilder kissed the top of her head.

"Can I go home now?" Violet asked.

"If that's what you want," Cree answered.

"I do." She took another deep breath and then stood.

Wilder rose, too. "You're going to have to go and talk with Luke and Damon, Lil…Violet."

"I will, but it's late and I'm too tired right now."

"Promise me you won't put off talking to the sheriffs, sweetness," Wilder demanded.

Violet spun to face him and poked him in the chest. "You don't get to order me around."

"I wasn't trying to order you around, but if you want these bastards caught and put behind bars, you have to tell someone what happened. If you don't want to talk with Luke and Damon, you can always come to us."

"I'll think about it." Violet glanced about the room and when she spotted her purse up on the dresser walked over and grabbed it. "Thank you for taking care of me."

Before Wilder could reply she raced down the hall and out the front door, slamming it closed behind her.

"Fuck!" Cree slammed his fist into the doorjamb before turning and racing toward the door. Wilder and Nash were on his heels. They all stepped out onto the porch and watched Lilac until she was safe inside before turning to enter their own home.

Wilder sighed and scrubbed a hand over his face. "Fuck is right!"

"Do you think we should call Luke?" Nash asked.

Wilder shook his head as he headed toward the fridge and snagged three beer bottles before handing two of them to his brothers. "We need to give her time to get her head around everything. If she hasn't talked to them by Monday, we can step in."

"She's not going to let us in after tonight." Cree sighed.

"What makes you think that?" Nash frowned.

"You didn't see how she wouldn't meet our gazes after telling us what her real name is?" Wilder asked.

"Shit! Yeah, I noticed." Nash rubbed the back of his neck. "Do you think she's going to take off?"

Wilder shook his head. "She's a part owner of the diner." Even as he spoke those words, he wasn't sure he believed them.

He hoped like hell that he and his brothers got the chance to court Lilac…Violet into having a relationship with them.

Chapter Five

As soon as she opened her eyes and blinked the sleep from her gaze, she glanced at the clock and gasped with amazement. It was almost eleven o'clock in the morning and she only had a couple of hours until she needed to get to the diner. She flung the covers aside and headed for the shower. As she stood under the warm water she thought of Enya. She hoped her friend wasn't annoyed that she hadn't been there at four like she usually was to help her with the baking.

Normally Violet went back home just as the breakfast rush was hitting and then returned to the diner for the lunch and dinner crowd. Yesterday, she and Delta had swapped their schedules since Delta's men had wanted to spend the morning with her.

As she dried off she thought of her mother. She couldn't believe she'd forgotten how those men had broken into their home and then beaten her mother to death. At the time she'd thought her mother had fallen asleep, but now that she remembered she knew that wasn't the case. Her mother's eyes had been open and turned toward the ceiling, and she hadn't been breathing. Her lips had been blue. When a sob escaped her mouth, she quickly pushed her thoughts aside. There was no time to wallow in the past. She needed to get to the diner for her shift.

When she was ready she grabbed her purse as well as the keys to her house and hurried out. Her gaze immediately went to the house next door but she quickly shifted her eyes to the pavement and walked rapidly. Her mind was in turmoil and she felt as if she would break down at any moment, but she didn't have the time. She changed her thoughts to what was on the specials board for the day, but for the life of her she couldn't remember.

Half an hour later, her mind still spinning in circles, Violet entered the diner. The noise of people laughing and talking while they ate felt so surreal, and though she was crying inside, she drew in a deep breath and pushed her turmoil aside.

She forced a smile to her lips when she entered the diner kitchen and, after greeting the others, wrapped an apron around her waist and got to work. Cooking normally helped her to relax but not today. Her gut was churning with nausea and she was feeling very shaky.

"Are you okay, Lilac?" Delta signed.

Her first instinct was to correct Delta about her rightful name but that would bring on all sorts of questions she wasn't ready to answer. If she told Delta, Enya, and the other women working at the diner that she wasn't who she'd thought she was, would they look at her differently? She wondered if she would ever get used to being called by a different name, when and if she did finally reveal her true name.

"I'm fine," she answered and quickly turned back to the stove when Delta frowned.

"You don't look fine," Enya said as she glanced up from where she was mixing another batch of muffins.

Violet shrugged as she turned the steaks on the grill. She loved the industrial-sized stove where the pots were steaming, and although her stomach growled because of the tantalizing aromas, there was no way she could eat right now. Usually she had a piece of toast for breakfast before going about her normal routine, but as soon as she lifted the jelly-covered bread to her mouth, she started salivating and not because she was hungry. She'd dumped the piece of toast in the trash and slugged down her coffee before brushing her teeth and heading out.

Even though she worked through the lunch hour and had acknowledged Delta and Enya when they'd left, she had no idea what she'd said. The orders had slowed over the last half hour, and when she glanced at the clock on the wall she was surprised to see that it was almost closing time. Once she and Enya had decided to partner up with Delta, they'd lengthened the opening hours of the diner from seven till ten. She was weary to the bone and yet she knew she'd have trouble going to sleep. The thought of closing her eyes and seeing her mother lying beaten on the floor sent chills racing up and down her spine.

She glanced toward the door when Jaylynn brought another load of dirty dishes in.

"There are only a few people left and they've all finished their meals. Do you want me to help you clean up in here?"

Violet shook her head. "No, I'll deal with the kitchen. If you could make sure everything is refilled and cleaned out in the diner that would be great."

"Sure." Jaylynn smiled and began filling the dishwashers before she headed out. Once they were running, Violet put all the leftover food into containers, refrigerated them, and started cleaning down the stove and counters. Once that was done she started scrubbing out the large cooking pots. Usually Katie, Kiara, or Jaylynn helped in the kitchen, but tonight she needed the monotonous chore to help her unwind.

It didn't seem to matter that she'd had hours of uninterrupted sleep after leaving the Sheffields' house. Violet was so tired she could barely stand up straight. Jaylynn came back in just as Violet was drying the last pot.

"Everything's done. The floor's been mopped, the tables and chairs are clean, and everything is set up for tomorrow morning."

"Thanks, Jaylynn. Why don't you head on home?" Violet suggested.

"Are you sure? I can stay if you want."

She shook her head and forced a tired smile. "Thanks anyway, but there's nothing left to do."

"Okay." Jaylynn smiled. "Do you want me to lock the front door?"

"No, I can do that when I leave."

Jaylynn nodded and waved. "See you tomorrow."

"Bye." Violet watched the other woman hurry away and then glanced up at the fridge where tomorrow's menu was written. Delta had covered the front of the glass industrial fridge with clear contact paper, which she thought was a great idea. Whiteboard markers were used and could be wiped off.

When she read over the list of dishes, she double-checked to make sure they had all the ingredients. Once Violet realized she was stalling, she sighed with resignation. There was no reason for her to hang around the diner any longer, but going back to her lonely cottage wasn't something she was looking forward to right now.

Violet was tired. Tired of being alone. Tired of being afraid. But she wasn't sure she was brave enough to reach out to anyone other than her new work partners and employees. If she could, she had a feeling she would breathe, eat, and sleep work twenty-four hours a day, and although she knew that wasn't healthy, she'd been doing just that for as long as she could remember.

She was twenty-five years old and had never celebrated her birthday beyond the first five years with her mom. That was sad in and of itself. Each year she'd nudged toward the age of sixteen had sent fear piercing her heart and soul. Ignoring the day she'd been born was easier to deal with.

After glancing about, she decided it was time to head out. She had half an hour's walk ahead of her, and if she couldn't sleep again, she would be up and back at the diner by four. It was already hedging toward midnight, and by the time she made it home, she would only get about three and a half hours of sleep under her belt.

Violet was used to dealing with the chores of the day with little to no sleep, but that didn't mean she wasn't exhausted to the bone. Some days she felt as if she was an eighty-year-old woman, or older. Since leaving that cult, all she ever had was herself and hard work, and she couldn't see that changing anytime soon.

After turning the lights off and locking up, she started for her little two-bedroom cottage. Each step she took hurt her feet after she'd been on them all day long, but she was used to that, too. As she walked along the deserted street, her mind drifted back to that horrible place she left behind ten years ago.

Twelve-year-old Lilac hurried to the kitchen after Messiah had ordered her, Fleur, and Rose to get dinner ready for everybody. She'd just grabbed some ingredients from the pantry when she heard grunting and moaning coming from the large living room. Thinking someone was sick and in pain, she raced toward the doorway and froze.

Sara-Jane, one of the five women living there, was down on all fours on the living room rug, to Violet's shock, totally naked. However, what horrified her more was the fact that she wasn't the only naked person in the room. She was surrounded by four adult men, and they were all as bare as the day they'd been born. What horrified Lilac was that the four men were all running their hands over Sara-Jane's body. It took her a few moments to get past her shock, and when she did she felt sick to her stomach. Sara-Jane shifted, and that was when Lilac saw that the poor woman was being used by three men at once. At first she thought Sara-Jane was on board with what the men were doing to her, but when she saw tears rolling down the woman's face, Lilac realized she wasn't.

She'd spun on her heels so fast she'd almost fallen over. After she'd regained her balance, Lilac had rushed to the trash can and puked her guts out. From that moment on, Lilac had lived in fear. Every time one of the men or older boys looked in her direction, she'd felt sick to her stomach.

A few years later after hearing Fleur and Rose crying in their beds, Lilac had known she was next and she'd begun to plan her escape. Hearing Virgil claiming her without her consent had solidified her need to leave.

Violet blinked and wiped at her cheeks when she felt something tickle over her skin. Her hands came away wet, and she stared at the moisture on her fingers incomprehensively for a second, until she realized she was crying. She knew she'd never be able to look back without getting emotional or feeling sick to her stomach, but at least she'd managed to escape.

The hair on her nape prickled, but when she glanced around she didn't see anyone. She picked up her pace, and five minutes later she was almost home. When she heard a truck rumbling up behind her, fear skittered up her spine, her breath hitched in her throat, and her heart slammed against her sternum.

Violet took off running and didn't stop until she was on her small porch, her hand digging into her purse as she searched for her keys. When the truck slowed and the lights shone over her and her door, she sobbed with fear and her purse fell from her hand. She turned slowly and pressed her back against the door, praying that whoever was here wasn't who she thought it was.

"Lilac…Violet, what's wrong?"

Violet's knees buckled and she slid down the door, landing on her ass with a thump. Relief made her muscles weak and she started shaking.

"Fuck, sweetness, what happened?" Wilder asked as he crouched in front of her.

She flinched automatically when he reached toward her.

"Did someone hurt you, honey?" Cree asked.

She shook her head and drew in a deep breath after deep breath as she tried to calm her racing heart and shaky limbs.

"Did someone scare you, baby?" Nash asked.

Finally, the adrenaline wore off and embarrassment set in. "I'm fine."

"That's the biggest fucking lie I've ever heard." Wilder snapped and then grasped her upper arms before helping her back to her feet. He nudged her purse with his toe and gazed at Cree. "Find her house keys."

"I can do it."

Wilder didn't answer nor did he let her go. He gazed into her eyes and then he swept her up into his arms. "I don't know what's going on with you, sweetness, but we're not leaving until we find out."

Violet wanted to scream at him and his brothers to leave her alone, but she remained silent. She was so on edge she was scared to open her mouth. She'd already told these men and the sheriffs part of her story, and while she'd felt better afterward, right now she was feeling scared and vulnerable. She'd never let on to anyone how she felt, and she had a feeling if she told them what had upset her, they'd never leave her alone again. So she decided the best offense was to remain silent.

She didn't notice she'd closed her eyes until she heard her keys in the lock and though she wanted to look up at Wilder, Cree, and Nash, she kept them closed. It felt so good to be in Wilder's arms, to have his warmth seeping into her cold body, and to have his arms around her as if he cared for her. She wanted to stay there forever.

Violet was tired and achy and still trembling, albeit only slightly, but she hoped that Wilder couldn't feel her shivering.

She inhaled raggedly and shuddered when he sat down with her in his lap. When he brushed his thumbs under her eyes, wiping the tears she didn't realize were still rolling down her cheeks, some of the cold in her heart faded.

"Look at me, Lil...Violet," Wilder demanded.

She shook her head. "Just let me go. Please?"

His hands cupped her face, and when he rested his forehead against hers, she shivered again. But this time it wasn't because she was cold or scared. Liquid desire pooled low in her belly, her heart rate sped up, as did her breathing. She was so tempted to press her lips against his to find out if they were as soft as they looked.

"Violet, we're trying to help you, baby," Nash said as he sat on the sofa next to her and Wilder. He laced his fingers with hers and squeezed.

She glanced over at Cree when he knelt in front of her, one of his big hands braced on her leg just above her knee.

Wilder nudged her gaze back to his. "Why are you trembling, sweetness? What were you running from?"

She wasn't sure what to say, so she licked her suddenly dry lips and shrugged.

"If you're in danger we need to know, honey," Cree said. "We can't protect you if we don't know who or what we're protecting you from."

"There is no danger," she answered breathily, and she mentally cursed.

"That's the biggest lie you've told tonight," Wilder said angrily. "As of Monday, we are deputies. It's our job to keep everyone in this town, this county safe. Please, talk to us, sweetness."

"I'm just being paranoid."

"But what if you're not?" Nash asked. "What if you are in danger? We can't help you unless you tell us what's going on."

With a sigh of resignation, Violet gripped Wilder's wrists and tugged his hands from her face. She braced a hand on Cree's shoulder, rose, and moved away from them. Cree got up from the floor and sat on the other side of Wilder.

"I'd just had a flash back to when…the hair on the back of my neck stood on end. I felt as if someone was watching me."

"Is that why you ran when you heard the truck?" Nash asked.

Violet nodded. She wrapped her arms around her waist and shivered when another shudder raced up her spine. When she glanced over at the Sheffield men and saw the concern on their faces, her heart filled with warmth. They seemed genuinely worried for her. She'd never had anyone concerned about her before and it made her feel special, cherished even. When she realized where her thoughts were heading she quickly pushed them aside.

"From now on, one or all of us will take you to and pick you up from the diner," Cree stated emphatically. "It's too dangerous for a single woman to be walking the streets alone in the wee hours of the morning."

"There's no need—"

"There's every need," Wilder snarled as he stood. "We care for you, Violet. We want to make sure you get home safe each and every night."

"I've been looking after myself—"

"You think we don't fucking know that," Cree said as he shoved to his feet. "We hate that you've been on your own for so fucking long."

"Why?" Violet cried. "You don't even know me."

Wilder stalked toward her, and as she took a step back, she glanced over at Nash and Cree. They were both moving toward her, too. Her heart flipped in her chest, and she gulped in a deep breath as she took another step back. Heated excitement coursed through her blood, and though she wanted to order them to leave, she couldn't seem to get her tongue to work. She licked her dry lips and crossed her arms over her chest. A soft moan escaped from her mouth when her arms brushed over her hard, aching nipples.

Her pussy and clit were throbbing and her panties were damp with need. When Wilder stopped a few feet in front of her, she glanced up into his heated green eyes. His collar-length black hair was curled up at the ends and she had the weirdest urge to touch it. She wanted to know if it felt as soft and silky as it looked.

Wilder, Cree, and Nash were identical triplets, but she could tell them apart easily. Cree had a scar running through his right eyebrow, and Nash had a beauty spot just under his left eye. Wilder's nose was slightly crooked as if it had been broken. Other than those discernible marks, there was no other way for a person to differentiate between them, but she didn't think she'd have any trouble telling them apart. They all smelled differently, and while she wasn't sure if that was because they used different bathing products or cologne, they each had an individual scent.

Wilder's fragrance was a mix of sandalwood and musky male. Cree's aroma was more like a spicy citrus scent, and Nash smelled like he'd just stepped out of a pine forest. Violet could have spent the rest of her life breathing in their individual essences, but when she had all three of them so close, she felt as if she was drowning in their masculine perfumes. Each time she breathed them in, she felt more and more drawn to them.

She blinked and tried to keep her mind on track, but it was one of the hardest things she'd ever had to do. Violet wanted to reach out and touch them. She wanted to know what it would be like to be kissed by each of them.

"We are trying to change that, sweetness," Wilder said in a husky voice.

"What?" She frowned.

"We are trying to get to know you, baby." Nash stepped to Wilder's right.

"We are very attracted to you, honey," Cree rasped out.

"We want to have a relationship with you, Violet."

Chapter Six

Wilder's stomach clenched when Violet shook her head, but when she met his gaze again, he saw a brief flash of longing cross her gorgeous mauve-colored eyes. He'd been yearning to kiss her since the first time he'd set eyes on her and had intended to give her some time to get to know him and his brothers, but he couldn't wait a second longer.

He stepped closer until there was scant space between their bodies, and then he palmed her face between his hands and tilted her head up to his. When she licked her lips again, he groaned and then breached the distance between them.

Every single muscle in his body tightened as he brushed his lips back and forth over Violet's. He took his time, easing her into the kiss, worried about scaring her off. However, when she moaned, her lips parting with the sound, triumphant excitement raced through his blood. His cock, which always seemed to be at half-mast whenever in her presence, twitched in his pants and then filled with blood.

He licked into her mouth, rubbing his tongue along hers before dancing around in her mouth. His hard cock jerked when she whimpered and when he felt her small hands wrapping themselves into his cotton shirt as she clutched the material. Wilder was so hot he felt as if he was burning alive. He shivered as heat raced up his spine and shifted on his feet when he felt lightning zinging through his body. She was at least a foot shorter than him and his brothers, and when the muscles in his lower back twinged at the awkward angle he was bent in, he lowered his hands from her face, wrapped his arms around her waist, and lifted her feet from the floor.

Violet moaned as she looped her arms around his neck and hooked her legs around his hips. Wilder pressed into her harder and groaned when his hard dick throbbed against her toned, flat belly. When she twirled her tongue around his, pre-cum leaked from the tip of his cock. He was so hungry for her, he wanted to strip her down and sink into her hot, wet cunt until he was balls-deep.

When she started rocking her hips against his stomach, he shifted his hold from her waist to her ass, kneading the muscular, fleshy globes until she whimpered with need. Wilder broke the kiss before licking and nibbling his way across her jaw to her neck. He nipped at her earlobe and then sucked the delectable skin into his mouth to soothe the sting, before moving to that sweet spot just under the ear most women seemed to have.

She cried out when he laved and suckled on the flesh beneath her ear, and when he pressed his stomach firmly into the junction of her thighs, she screamed her release. Wilder shelfed her ass with his forearm and lifted his gaze up to her face.

He'd never seen a sexier sight than what he was seeing right now. Violet had her head tilted back against the wall, her mouth was gaping open, and there was a rosy hue to her normally pale cheeks. When her eyelids fluttered open, he nearly lost his wad. Her eyes were glazed over with residual passion, and they had darkened to an indigo color. She blinked and then glanced off to either side of him, and Wilder figured she was embarrassed when her cheeks got even rosier.

"You are the sexiest fucking woman I've ever seen. There is so much passion locked up inside of you, sweetness. Cree, Nash, and I want to explore this attraction that's between us."

Violet shook her head and lowered her eyes, but Wilder wasn't about to let her hide from him or his brothers after what they'd just shared. She was so damn special and his gut was telling him that she was the woman they'd been waiting for. He couldn't let her go now that they'd just found her. He wanted to spend all his free time with

Violet so they could get to know each other, to build a relationship that would last forever.

"You'd better not deny the attraction, Violet, not after what we've just shared."

"I can't do this," she whispered tremulously.

"Why the hell not?" Nash asked.

"Because men only ever dish out pain," Violet yelled.

"We have no idea what you've dealt with in the past, baby," Cree began, "but I can guaran-damn-tee we would *never*, *ever*, do anything to hurt you."

"All of us have emotional scars, sweetness, but you can't let that hold you back. We've seen some pretty fucked-up shit after serving in the Marines and we've only had each other to rely on. We all lost our parents when we were young, too, but we've never given up hope of finding someone to settle down and build a life with."

"I-I don't know...I..."

"Take a breath, baby." Cree reached over, pried her fingers from Wilder's shirt, and laced them with his.

Nash clasped her other hand.

"I don't know if I can do this."

Wilder sighed as he lowered her feet to the floor. "Why, Violet? What are you so scared of?"

When he realized she was shaking, he grew more concerned. He held her hips to keep her on her feet as she swayed. Wilder was scared she was about to pass out because all that rosy color had leeched from her cheeks. Her eyes were dilated but not from passion this time. Violet was absolutely terrified, and it made him think that they may not have a chance with her after all.

"They used to rape the women," Violet whispered in a ragged voice.

Red-hot rage hazed over his eyes, and for a moment he thought he was going to lose his shit. But their woman was already scared enough and there was no fucking way he was adding to her fear.

However, he and his brothers needed to talk to her, to reassure her again that they would never in a million years hurt her. He glanced at Cree and Nash and saw they were barely containing their anger. Both his brothers had their jaws clenched and their lips pulled into a tight angry line.

Wilder moved carefully as he wrapped his arm around her waist again. His heart ached when she blinked up at him with astonishment, and he mentally cursed when she quickly lowered her gaze to his chest. He'd seen the sheen of tears in those amazing lilac-colored eyes.

"Come and sit down so we can talk, sweetness."

"What's there to talk about?" Violet muttered under her breath, but he heard her.

Wilder guided her over to the small two-seater sofa and glanced at his brothers as they sat in the armchairs across from them.

"Who was raped, baby?" Nash asked in a low gentle voice as if he was worried a louder voice would frighten her.

"The women," she said and then inhaled raggedly. "There were five women living at that place and us three girls. The rest were men and teenage boys. The men raped the women whenever they felt like it and the teenage boys raped the two girls."

Wilder wanted to roar his rage to the ceiling, but he swallowed his anger down and shifted closer to Violet. He tentatively placed his hand between her shoulder blades and almost sighed with relief when she didn't react to his touch. He'd been worried she would flinch away from him. He began to caress up and down her back over her shirt, hoping to convey what little comfort he could. He gazed at Nash when his brother sat forward in his seat, and when he opened his mouth, Wilder shook his head. They all needed to remain silent so that she would finish what she was about to tell them.

"None of us were allowed to be naïve," Violet said. "We were taught about sex from the age of eight years old. Messiah made us girls watch movies of people having sex. I was horrified and tried to run from the room, but he had one of his...friends standing in the doorway so I couldn't leave. He said that Messiah wanted us to learn how to please a man so that when we were older we would know what to do."

"Fucking sick bastards," Cree snarled before he shoved from his seat and began to pace.

Wilder was so angry he wanted to punch something but he stayed where he was.

"I sat in that room and watched as a woman was taken by three men at the same time. Fleur and Rose were with me, and when I glanced over at them, they didn't seem to be concerned. Maybe it was natural curiosity or maybe they were so terrified they weren't game to look away from the TV screen. It got too much and I ended up closing my eyes."

"Thank God," Nash said hoarsely.

Violet shook her head. "The asshole must have been told to make sure we watched, because the next thing I knew he was lifting me from the cushion and when he sat back down he put me in his lap."

"Motherfucker," Wilder spat out. He tensed and met Violet's gaze worried his outburst would upset her, but thankfully, she nodded in agreement.

"He held my face so I couldn't look away and made us watch until the movie was finished."

Wilder was so full of rage his hands were shaking, but he tried to keep his ire from showing. First thing in the morning he was going to see Luke and Damon. These people were so fucking sick they needed to be behind bars.

"Did they make you do that often?" Cree asked.

Violet nodded. "On the fourth Sunday of every month."

"Fuck!" Nash ran his fingers through his hair.

"Not long after I'd just turned twelve, Fleur, Rose, and I were starting to prepare dinner, but when I heard strange noises coming from the living room, I thought someone was sick or hurt and went to investigate. No matter how hard I try I can't get that image out of my mind."

Wilder wrapped an arm around her shoulders and eased her against his side when her trembling got worse. She leaned against him and shivered as if she was cold to the bones, but he was happy that she didn't try to pull away.

"What did you see, honey?" Cree asked.

"Four men having sex with one woman. I didn't realize what they were doing at first because I was too shocked at seeing them all naked, but when I did, I started to feel sick. Sara-Jane was crying and looked as if she was in pain, but she just let them do what they wanted. She didn't make a sound or try to fight them. I ran back to the kitchen and threw up. Why? Why wouldn't she have tried to fight them off?"

Wilder's heart cracked when she turned to face him. Tears were rolling down her cheeks and her lips were trembling. "I don't know, sweetness."

"She let them rape her," Violet yelled and then she was sobbing her heart out.

Wilder lifted her onto his lap and wrapped his arms around her as she cried. Her whole body shook with the heaving sobs coming from her mouth, and he had to blink back his own tears. He glanced over at Cree and Nash to see they were also struggling with their emotions.

Guilt assailed him. No wonder Violet didn't want to have a relationship. She had to have been scared out of her fucking mind while he'd ravished her mouth. He rocked back and forth as she bawled her eyes out, and he hoped that he hadn't fucked everything up by moving too soon.

Please, God, please don't let me have ruined everything.

After what seemed like forever, Violet's tears slowed and finally stopped until she was hiccupping and gasping for breath. He kept caressing her back and rocking until her breathing slowed. When he gazed down at her and noticed she had her eyes closed, he thought she'd fallen asleep, but then her eyes fluttered open.

"I'm sorry. All I ever seem to do when I'm around you all, is cry."

Wilder cupped her face and swiped his thumb over her tearstained cheek. "Don't ever apologize for having a heart, sweetness. You have so much pain stored up, it needs to be purged."

She nodded and licked her lips. "I need a drink."

"I'll get it, baby." Nash shoved to his feet and raced toward the kitchen. He was back moments later with a glass of water and a box of tissues.

"Thanks," Violet said as she pulled some tissues from the box and then drank the water down in one go.

Wilder hated to ask the question on his lips, but he needed to know if he and his brothers stood a chance with her. "Do you think we'd hurt you, Violet?"

"No," she answered.

"That's right, sweetness. I would rather cut off my own arm or rip out my own heart before I ever hurt you."

"That goes for me, too," Cree said.

"And me," Nash stated.

"I know deep down that none of you or any of the men in this town would ever hurt someone weaker than they are, but after what I lived with, it's sometimes hard to believe that I'm safe."

"Did I scare you when I was kissing you, Violet?" Wilder caressed his thumb over her cheek. Her skin was so soft he couldn't seem to stop touching her.

"Not at first."

"Were you scared when Wilder made you come, honey?" Cree frowned.

"What did we do that frightened you, sweetness?" Wilder asked.

"It's nothing you did."

"Explain why you were scared then, baby." Nash rubbed the back of his neck.

"When you were all crowding me, I had a flashback of what happened to Sara-Jane. It had nothing to do with…" Violet waved her hands in the air and blushed.

"So you aren't afraid we'd hurt you?" Cree asked.

Wilder tensed as he waited for Violet's answer. When he looked at Cree and Nash, he saw that they were in the same boat. They both had their hands clenched into fists.

"No."

He released the air in his lungs on a long, slow exhale and the tension in his muscles eased.

"We still want to spend time with you, sweetness, but we are willing to ease back and go at your pace."

Wilder frowned when she swallowed audibly and once more waited with bated breath as she thought over what he'd just said.

"I thought I left all that fear behind, you know. When I caught a glimpse of the guy that looked like Virgil, it brought everything back. I hate being scared. I don't want to spend the rest of my life living with terror."

"What are you saying, baby?" Nash asked.

"I-I think…I'd like…to spend time with you all."

Wilder wanted to shout with joy, but he smiled instead. He couldn't believe how fucking brave Violet was. She was so fucking strong. What other fifteen-year-old girl would have run away and traveled all alone? She'd put herself through school and college, and although she'd lived in an abusive household, she'd survived and waited for her chance to escape. That told him she wasn't as fragile as she appeared. In fact, she was stronger than a lot of the soldiers he'd toured overseas with. Violet may be reserved and scared, but she hadn't let her fear rule how she lived her life.

"Thank you, sweetness. I promise you we will never do anything to intentionally hurt you. We may fuck up from time to time, but as long as we keep our lines of communication open, I think we'll be able to build a relationship with strong foundations."

Violet gave him a tentative smile and nodded.

He could still see the uncertainty and wariness in those gorgeous mauve eyes, but it was up to him and his brothers to put her at ease.

He didn't care if it took them years to earn her trust because he knew without a shadow of a doubt that Violet was worth it.

He was already falling hard and fast for her.

Chapter Seven

Violet was exhausted and could barely keep her eyes open. She was emotionally and physically drained, yet she felt better than she had for a long while. She'd finally told someone about the horrors of her childhood, and instead of looking at her horrified, as if she had two heads or something, Wilder, Cree, and Nash had all been angry on her behalf. Oh, they'd tried to hide their rage, but she'd have to have been blind to miss the fury in their eyes. She covered her mouth when she yawned and was about to remove her hand when she yawned, right on top of the last one.

"You're exhausted, sweetness. It's time we left you so you can crawl into bed."

She glanced at her watch and was surprised to see it was almost one thirty in the morning. No wonder she was so tired, but the thought of being alone when Virgil could be hiding out somewhere scared her to death.

Wilder stood with her in his arms, waiting until she was steady on her feet, and then removed his hands from her waist. He leaned down, kissed her on the forehead, and turned toward the door.

"Don't go. Please?" She cringed when she heard the tremor in her own voice.

"What are you saying, baby?" Nash approached slowly, frowning.

"I'm scared."

Cree scrubbed a hand down his face. "You're scared of being alone?"

Violet nodded and lowered her gaze to the floor.

"Do you want me to stay with you, sweetness?" Wilder asked.

She lifted her eyes to his. "Would you?"

"If that's what you want, of course I will, Violet."

"This doesn't mean…I'm not going to…"

"Hey." Wilder clasped her hand and tugged her against him. "I won't do anything but hold you in my arms while you sleep. Okay?"

"Okay." She sighed out her answer, relief surging through her that he didn't think she was offering more to him.

"Me and Cree are going to head out, baby." Nash stroked a finger down her face.

She nodded and smiled, but called him back when he turned away. "Cree?"

"Yes, Violet."

"Thank you for tonight."

"Don't thank me, honey. It was my pleasure to be with you." He clasped and lifted her hand to his mouth, kissing the back of it before walking toward the door.

Nash cupped her chin in his hand, tilted her face up to his, and kissed her forehead. "Sleep well, baby. We'll see you tomorrow. Yeah?"

"Yeah." Violet watched as they left and wondered how she'd been lucky enough to find such kind, caring men. She still couldn't get her head around the fact that they were attracted to her and wanted to have a relationship with her. Excitement fluttered in her belly, but the small adrenaline burst was short-lived. She was too tired to think anymore.

"Let me lock up while you get ready for bed, sweetness. I'll be there in a few minutes. All right?"

Violet nodded and stepped back when Wilder released her. She hurried toward her bedroom. After gathering a clean pair of sleeping shorts and tank top, she entered the bathroom to use the facilities and got changed. She washed her hands and face, brushed her teeth, and fiddled with the tie in the end of her hair. Usually she slept with her hair down since it had to be bound all the time while working with food, but she wasn't sure if she should. What if her hair got in Wilder's face? Would he be annoyed or angry with her?

"Are you okay, Violet?" Wilder asked through the closed door.

She startled so badly her feet left the floor and she hit her hip on the edge of the bathroom counter hard enough to make her gasp.

Wilder burst through the door, and after glancing about to make sure she was safe, he walked over to her. "What's wrong, sweetness? I heard you gasp with pain."

"Oh. I um…" She lowered her gaze to the floor, but then she tilted her head up and met his gaze. "You surprised me when you spoke and I ended up hitting my hip on the corner of the counter.

"Do you want me to take a look?" Wilder frowned. "I can get you some ice?"

"It's fine."

"If you're sure." He quirked an eyebrow.

"I'm okay."

"Why don't you get under the covers, sweetness? I'll be out in a minute. Okay?"

"Sure." Violet hurried toward the door and closed it behind her. She switched on a bedside lamp and got into bed. She stared at the ceiling for a moment, but then she turned until her back was to the bathroom door and gnawed on her lip. She was nervous about sleeping with a man even though she knew Wilder wouldn't do anything unless she wanted him to. It was tempting, after the kisses they'd shared earlier, but she wasn't ready to take the next step. Even though he'd blown her mind by giving her an orgasm, she was still a little wary. Hopefully, she would be able to relax around him, Cree, and Nash when she got to know them better.

She held her breath when the bathroom door opened, and tensed when she heard rustling. Was he taking his clothes off? Violet didn't know what to do. The urge to get out of bed was strong, but then she remembered how kind and gentle he and his brothers had been with her. They'd been horrified over the things she'd seen when she was a child, but not once had they tried to force themselves on her.

Her heart knew she was safe with the Sheffield men, but she needed to give her mind time to catch up.

"I'm going to leave my boxers and T-shirt on. Okay, sweetness? If you want I can sleep in my jeans and on top of the covers so you're comfortable. Or if you'd prefer I can sleep in the spare room or on the sofa."

Violet rolled to her other side so she could see Wilder. His jeans were undone, so the movement she'd heard had to be when he was taking his shoes off. "You wouldn't fit on the sofa and I don't have a spare bed in the other bedroom. You'll get too hot if you sleep in your jeans."

"So you're okay if I take them off?" he asked.

Violet bit her lip and nodded.

"Thank you, love."

She closed her eyes when he shifted closer to the bed, and while she was tempted to peek when she heard him lower the zipper, she squeezed her lids down tighter. A breeze drifted over her skin when he lifted the covers, and she held her breath as he got into bed.

She jerked when his hand caressed over her shoulder and opened her eyes.

"You need to relax, sweetness. Are you sure you want me to sleep in your bed? I don't mind sleeping on the floor."

"I want you here, Wilder. I feel safe with you and your brothers. I'm just a little nervous because I've never shared a bed with anyone before."

"Never?" Wilder asked in a hoarse voice.

Violet knew he was asking more than just about sharing a bed. "Never," she answered honestly.

"Come here, darlin'." Wilder lifted his arm, and when she scooted closer he wrapped it around her shoulders.

She rested her head in the crook of his arm and inhaled his delectable cologne and manly scent. "You smell nice."

Wilder chuckled. "I'm glad you like the way I smell, sweetness. You smell good enough to eat."

"That's because I'm cooking food all the time."

"That's not what I meant. I can smell your perfume, body wash, or shampoo and the natural scent you give off. It's a delicious combination."

"Uh. Okay, if you say so." She yawned.

"Close your eyes, sweetness. You're safe with me."

Violet relaxed and closed her eyes and drifted to sleep in seconds.

* * * *

"Is Violet okay? Did you call Luke and Damon to set up a meeting?" Nash asked the second Wilder walked into the kitchen.

He'd heard Wilder enter the house just before eleven and had been on pins waiting for him to finish in the shower.

"She's fine."

"Did she have any nightmares?" Cree asked as he poured coffee into three mugs.

"No."

"Did you talk her into coming over for lunch?"

"Yes. She'll be here around one, and yes, she agreed to tell Luke and Damon what she told us last night."

"Thank fuck. Those bastards need to be locked behind bars for the rest of their lives," Nash said angrily.

"They fucking do," Cree agreed.

"They need to be fucking castrated as well as have their dicks cut off," Wilder snarled.

"Did you get to talk about anything else?" Nash asked.

"No. Violet's not really a morning person."

"What do you mean?" Cree frowned.

"She didn't speak a word until she'd finished her first cup of coffee. She just sat at the kitchen counter and stared off into space."

Nash grinned. "I can just imagine that. Did she sleep with her hair up or down?"

"Up. I wanted to tell her to take it down, but she was nervous and I didn't want to push her," Wilder explained.

"Why was she nervous? She asked you to stay." Cree sipped his coffee.

Nash gazed at Wilder expectantly as he took a swig of coffee, too.

"She's never slept with anyone before."

Coffee spewed from Nash's mouth, and he coughed and spluttered as he choked.

Nash laughed uproariously, and Wilder chuckled.

"You all right there, Bro?" Cree asked when he'd stopped laughing.

Nash gave Cree the finger but smiled. "Does that mean what I think it means?" He asked when he had his breath back.

"Yes."

"She told you she was a virgin?" Cree asked.

"Not in so many words," Wilder answered. "I knew she wasn't experienced when we started kissing. She didn't know what to do at first and tentatively copied what I did. When she stopped thinking and let the passion take over…well, you both saw what happened."

"She has so much fire hidden in that small body," Nash said.

"Shit yeah, she does." Cree sighed.

"Just don't go pushing her." Wilder pointed at first Cree and then Nash.

Nash scowled at his brother. "You were the one pushing last night, Wilder."

"Yeah, I know and it scared the shit out of me when she said she couldn't continue. I thought I fucked up everything."

"Thank fuck she didn't kick us out." Cree rubbed his hands together.

"There is that," Nash said. "She's a very forgiving, loving person."

"Let's just hope we can get her to love us," Wilder said.

"One day at a time, Bro." Nash clapped Wilder on the shoulder.

"Yeah, one day at a time." Wilder nodded.

* * * *

Violet sucked in a deep breath and exhaled before she knocked on the door.

Just as Cree opened the door, a truck turned into the driveway. "Hi, honey. Come on in."

She nodded and stepped over the threshold and glanced about the living room. She was too nervous to take much in and for a moment wished she hadn't agreed to talk to the sheriff, but then she mentally shook her head. If she didn't tell the officers what she'd seen when she was a kid, that would mean those sick assholes would be getting away with rape, let alone murder and abduction, and god knew what else they'd done. For all she knew, those bastards were still kidnapping kids from their homes, from their beds, and enslaving them on the cult land.

It was way over time for Violet to make a statement so those pricks could be charged, stand trial, and be locked behind bars.

"What are you doing out here, baby?" Nash asked as he entered the living room.

"I wasn't sure whether to wait for Cree."

"Cree's big and ugly enough to take care of himself, Violet. Come on into the kitchen."

She couldn't help but giggle over Nash's earlier statement. When Nash had insulted Cree, he was also insulting himself since they were identical.

"That's a sound I would love to hear more of." Nash clasped her hand in his and guided her into the other room.

"Hey, sweetness." Wilder smiled at her as if he hadn't seen her for days let alone a couple of hours. "Did you get your laundry done?"

"Yes."

"That's good." Nash winked. "Does that mean you have the rest of the day free?"

"It does." Violet smiled shyly.

"Was that you I heard laughing, Violet?"

She nodded.

"Care to share the joke?" Wilder cocked his eyebrow expectantly.

Her heart thumped against her ribs, her areolae contracted, and her pussy clenched. Wilder, Nash, and Cree were so damn sexy they sent her blood racing through her veins with so much ease. She wondered if Wilder realized how just a simple quirk of an eyebrow got her juices flowing. She shook her head. Just being in the same room as the three tall, sexy, muscular, handsome men had her body responding.

"What's wrong, baby?" Nash frowned.

"Nothing," she answered honestly. She wasn't about to let on how they affected her because she already felt as if she was in over her head and didn't want to give them any more ammunition against her. She quickly pushed that thought aside. None of the Sheffield men were dishonest or sly. They'd already proven how trustworthy they were.

"I laughed because when Nash insulted Cree he was also insulting you and himself because you all look the same."

"You don't have any trouble telling us apart though, do you, baby?" Nash stated more than asked.

"I don't."

"How can you differentiate between us so easily when others have so much trouble?" Wilder asked.

"You have a slightly crooked nose." Violet lifted her hand, stroked a finger down his nose, and then met Nash's gaze. "You have a beauty spot under your left eye, and Cree has a scar dissecting the middle of his right eyebrow."

"You're a very observant young lady," Sheriff Luke Sun-Walker said as he entered the room behind Cree.

When she saw the other two big men with the sheriff, Violet sidled closer to Nash. "It's okay, baby. These men won't hurt you."

"Let me through, you big oafs." A small, slim, dark-haired woman shoved her way through the men and smiled when she saw Violet. "Hi, you must be Lilac. I'm Felicity Eagle Sun-Walker, but please call me Flick."

"Hi," Violet responded shyly.

"Actually, this is Violet Evans." Nash wrapped an arm around Violet's shoulders.

She scowled up at Nash before meeting Flick's gaze again. "You can call me Lilac."

"What do you prefer to be called?" Flick asked.

Violet gnawed on her lip as she thought about her reply and then answered, "Violet or Vi is fine."

"Vi it is." Flick smiled and then pointed to the other men. "You already know, Luke, but these two sexy giants are Tom and Billy Eagle, my other husbands."

"Hello," she greeted.

"Hi, guys." Wilder shook each man's hand and then moved aside so Nash could do the same. They nodded and smiled at Felicity.

Nash moved forward, taking Violet with him, and shook each man's hand.

"Have you remembered more, Lil...Violet?" Luke asked.

Violet nodded.

"Do you want to tell me now, or after lunch?"

When Violet pressed her hands against her stomach as if she felt ill, Nash frowned. He hoped she wasn't so nervous or upset she was getting sick, and while he would have suggested she get the difficult part of the day over before eating, he held his tongue. This was her decision to make, and she didn't need any interference from him or his brothers. She glanced at Billy, Tom, and then Flick before meeting Luke's gaze again. "Now."

"Why don't we go into the living room?" Nash suggested.

"Before you go." Flick held up a finger. "Do you need any help with anything?"

Cree nodded. "If you want, you could make a tossed salad. Everything else is ready."

"Okay. Tom, Billy, you can help me," Flick ordered as she walked toward the fridge and tugged the door open.

"Sure thing, sugar." Billy smiled and winked at Violet and then took the salad ingredients Felicity shoved into his arms.

"Are you sure you're up to this, baby?" Nash asked as he guided Violet into the living room.

She clutched at his hand with her cold, trembling one. "It's well past time something was done about those assholes. If I don't speak up, they're going to continue to…hurt women and children."

"Me, Wilder, and Cree will stay by your side. Okay? If you need a break, just tell us and we'll stop."

"I need to do this, Nash. I should have done this a long time ago." She frowned.

Nash settled her on the middle sofa cushion before sitting beside her. Wilder sat on her other side, and Cree sank to the floor in front of her, resting his back against her legs. Cree glanced at her over his shoulder. "Is this okay with you, honey?"

"Yeah," she sighed.

Luke glanced about the room, looking for a seat.

"If you need to sit close, I can bring a chair over," Wilder said.

"I can sit on the coffee table if that's all right with you," Luke replied and then met Violet's gaze. "I don't want you to be uncomfortable, but I need to be able to record your statement on my phone. I'll have it typed up and you can sign it tomorrow."

"Okay," Violet said.

"You're a very strong, brave woman, Violet," Luke said as he pulled his phone from his pocket.

Violet shrugged as if she didn't believe the sheriff's statement but didn't say anything.

Nash hoped that she didn't get as upset as she had the night before because he wasn't sure his heart could take seeing her in so much pain. He just hoped that whatever she told Luke was enough to get the ball rolling to have the fuckers under lock and key for the rest of their lives. They were sick fucking monsters preying on young children and women. They were stealing children's innocence as well as sexually assaulting them and holding them hostage.

Rage coursed through Nash's body, and for the first time in his life he wanted to kill while no longer fighting in a war. However, that would mean they wouldn't suffer like they'd made Violet, those women, and the other girls suffer. He wanted to beat them senseless and leave them to endure untold pain. They needed to live the rest of their lives behind bars, and maybe one day they would realize what they'd done, how much agony they'd caused. But assholes like that didn't have a conscience. Those fuckers didn't care about anyone but themselves.

Nash just hoped that the man Violet had thought she'd seen wasn't the bastard from her past.

If he ever saw the prick, he wasn't sure he wouldn't kill him by ripping his fucking head from his neck.

Chapter Eight

"What's up with you, Lilac?" Delta asked. "You're very quiet."

Deciding to take the bull by the horns, Violet replied, "My birth name isn't Lilac."

She glanced over at Enya when the other woman gasped. Although she was a little embarrassed over blurting that out, she wasn't about to take it back since it was the truth.

"Why have you been using another name?" Cindy asked. "Are you in witness protection?"

Violet shook her head as she met each of the women's gazes. Delta had set up weekly meetings which always landed on a Monday since that was the quietest day for the diner. Jaylynn, Katie, Kiara, as well as Cindy, Enya, and Delta were all staring at her as if she'd just told them the moon was falling. Cindy was a godsend since she was a fluent signer, and while Violet and the other women were getting better, they still stumbled now and then.

"But you signed a contract." Delta frowned. "Does that mean it's not legal?"

"I have no idea," Violet responded and quickly went on to explain, "I didn't know my real name wasn't Lilac Primrose until a few days ago. I'm sorry, Delta. I didn't deceive you on purpose."

Enya, who was sitting beside her on the sofa, turned and clasped one of her hands in hers. "So, what's going on?"

Violet quickly explained the situation, summarizing her story so that she didn't take up all their meeting time.

"Oh. My. God." Delta signed. "Are you okay? Have you seen this guy since then? I'll get my lawyer to get another contract for you to sign. Have you been to the sheriffs? They need to know what's going on. Do we need to do anything different to protect you?"

"Whoa!" Violet held up her hands and forced a smile. "We don't need to change anything, Delta. For all I know, I was just being paranoid. There's no way that…man could know where I was."

"You're deluding yourself, Violet," Enya stated firmly. "People like that always manage to find their victims. Look what happened to Delta."

"Do you want to take some time off?" Delta asked. "We can handle things for a while."

Violet shook her head. "No, I need to work. Work is the only thing keeping me sane right now."

"I can understand that," Enya muttered, but Violet heard her. There was more to Enya than met the eye. The poor woman looked as exhausted as she felt. She wanted to ask if she was okay, but she didn't want to pry. Enya would open up with them in her own good time.

"Do you want to swap shifts with me?" Delta asked. "I don't think you should be walking home by yourself so late at night."

"Uh, I don't think that's going to be a problem," Violet hedged.

Cindy chuckled gaining everyone's attention. "Those sexy new deputies seemed to have taken a shine to our Violet. They dropped her off before they headed to the sheriff's department."

"Cindy!" Violet hoped that her face wasn't as red as it felt.

"Ha, you're attracted to them, too." Katie giggled.

"I am not," she quickly denied.

"And there's the proof." Enya smiled as she pointed at her.

"So what if I am." Violet threw her hands up in the air with exasperation. "It's not going to go anywhere."

"Why not?" Delta asked. "They're tall, muscular, and handsome. Why wouldn't you jump at the chance to have a relationship with them? Unless they just want to get into your pants."

"Delta!"

"What? I have to look after my partners and girls. If those guys are just trying to get you into bed, then you're better off without them."

"They don't."

"They don't want to take you to bed?" Jaylynn frowned. "What's wrong with them? Are they blind? You're gorgeous."

"That's not what I meant." Violet's lips twitched. It was wonderful having new friends willing to stick up for her. Tears filled her eyes, and she quickly blinked, trying to dispel them.

"What did they do?" Enya asked. "If those assholes have hurt you, I'm going to kick their asses, deputies or not."

"They haven't done anything, Enya. In fact, they've been very protective and kind."

"Then why the tears?" Kiara asked.

"They want a relationship with me," she replied.

"And?" Delta asked.

"I'm scared."

"Of what?" Cindy frowned. "They're not the sort of men to go around hurting women or breaking hearts on purpose."

Violet couldn't believe that Cindy was so perceptive at such a young age, but then she'd grown up in this town where polyamorous relationships were the norm and the men were possessive and protective. Maybe she'd learned by watching how the men treated their women.

"Of everything."

"You're going to have to be more specific, Lil…Violet," Enya said. "We're not leaving this room until you spill."

Violet closed her eyes and sucked in a deep breath, and then explained about being abducted and what it had been like growing up in a cult. When she finished, the silence in the room had her heart breaking. She glanced at the other women, expecting to see horror on their faces, but she was surprised to see sympathy and understanding.

"I totally understand where you're coming from," Delta said. "While our situations were different, I was scared, too. However, you can't spend the rest of your life on the outside looking in, Violet. You're missing out on so much. Being in love and being loved by a man, or in our case, men, is the most amazing experience of my life."

"Delta's right," Enya said. "Being loved, having someone to lean on when you need it, is wonderful. Don't throw something that could be special away because you're afraid. This could be the one and only time you meet the men of your dreams, and if you walk away from them, you could end up regretting it for the rest of your life."

Violet had a feeling Enya was talking from experience. The poor woman looked so sad and there was so much pain in her eyes. She pulled Enya into her arms and hugged her. "Thanks."

Enya squeezed her back and then drew from Violet's arms. "You're welcome."

"So, are you going to do it?" Cindy asked excitedly, practically bouncing in her seat.

"Yeah, are you?" Delta asked with a smile.

Violet gulped and then nodded.

All the woman cheered and laughed.

"You aren't making a mistake, Violet," Jaylynn said. "They're good men. Trust your instincts. They won't let you down."

Violet met each of the women's gazes and smiled. "Thank you, all of you."

"Don't thank us," Delta said. "This is what friends are for. Right, ladies?"

"Hell yes," they replied simultaneously and then erupted into laughter again.

Violet had never been more glad to have ended up in Slick Rock. It had been a blessing, and the benefits just kept coming.

She had wonderful new friends and was about to have a relationship with three men. *Three*! Although that was daunting, the others were right. She couldn't let fear stop her from finding out if she and the Sheffield brothers could have something special. She didn't want to have regrets and wonder about them for the rest of her life.

She was strong since she'd had to be. It was time to pull her big-girl panties up and face life head-on.

* * * *

Virgil couldn't believe what he was seeing. Everywhere he looked there were polyamorous couples. He rubbed his hands together as he chuckled. Lilac must be the slut he'd always thought she was to end up in this town. Had she known about the ménages before she'd arrived here? She had to have. She was such a fucking hypocrite.

He'd remembered seeing the distaste on her face when she'd been forced to watch the movies. Now here she was in the midst of promiscuity. It was laughable.

When he saw three deputies walking down the street toward him on the opposite side of the road, Virgil ducked down a narrow side alley and turned back toward the motel. Something else he'd noticed about this backward town was that the men were more observant than most. That was going to make his job harder, but he wasn't giving up until he had that slut under him. He couldn't wait to get his hands on her. She was supposed to have been his. She'd escaped a month or so before her sixteenth birthday, and while he'd been able to slake his lust with the other bitches, he couldn't get that slut off his mind.

He'd felt as if he'd failed. He'd never forget how angry his father had been that the cow had been able to escape while under his watch. His father had nearly burst a vein, but what had pissed him off and still irked him even after all these years was the ribbing he'd gotten from the other guys and men. They'd called him weak, including his fucked-up dad.

Virgil had shown the asshole he wasn't as weak as he'd thought when he killed the fucker. However, he knew he would never really have the respect of the other men at the commune until he'd proven he was their rightful leader. It didn't seem to matter that he ruled with an iron fist, figuratively and literally. His failure was hanging over his head and wouldn't go away until he had Lilac where she was supposed to be.

Back at the commune, tied to his bed where she belonged.

* * * *

The moment Cree spotted Violet, he knew something had changed. The shadows in her eyes were gone and she was smiling.

He, Wilder, and Nash had been busy all day long in their new deputy positions, and while he'd enjoyed the work, he hadn't been able to stop thinking about Violet. She was it for him and his brothers, and he hoped that she would end up accepting them into her life.

"She looks happy," Wilder said.

"Yeah." Cree shifted on his feet and adjusted his hardening cock to a more comfortable position.

"She's so fucking beautiful." Nash sighed as he threaded his fingers through his hair.

Cree was leaning against the side of the truck and straightened when Violet exited the diner. "Do you need some help, honey?"

She shook her head as she turned to the door and locked up before turning to face him and his brothers again. "Wow, look at all of you."

Cree held his arms out to the side and smiled. Her gaze wandered over his body from head to toe, pausing in strategic places before making the return journey. She glanced over at his brothers and ogled them the same way she'd just gawked at him.

"Y'all look so handsome, sexy, and tough in your uniforms and gun belts."

Cree stopped in front of her and nudged her chin up. "You think we're sexy?"

"Uh." Violet glanced away.

"You can't take it back, honey. It's far too late." Cree grinned when she frowned at him.

She cleared her throat and changed the subject. "How was your first day on the job?"

"It was good," Nash answered as Cree guided her to the truck.

"How was your day, sweetness?" Wilder asked as he held the passenger door open.

"Great!"

"You sound happy," Cree said as he got into the back with Violet.

"I am. I have some amazing friends."

"Yes, you do." Cree rubbed over the middle of his chest with his knuckles and then blew over them.

Violet chuckled. "You're such an idiot."

"Oh, you wound me, honey."

She laughed and slapped him on the arm.

Cree loved this playful side of Violet, and from the way his brothers were grinning from ear to ear, they did, too.

"You finished up earlier than we thought you would, baby," Nash said as he gazed at Violet over his shoulder.

"Mondays are the slowest work day for us. People tend to want to stay in after being out on the weekend and the start of the work week." Violet shrugged. "It's good for us though because we have a staff meeting every Monday and we go through the kitchen to see what we've used and order replacements. We also give the place a thorough cleaning."

"That makes sense." Nash nodded.

Cree hated that they'd arrived home all too soon. He didn't want Violet to say goodnight and head into her own home. He wanted to hold her in his arms, kiss, touch, and make love with her, but he wasn't going to push. She was already skittish and she needed time to get to know them more.

Wilder pulled into the driveway and turned the truck off. Cree got out and instead of racing around to the other side so he could help

Violet out, he let Nash deal with it. It wasn't that he didn't want to touch her, but he was so hungry for her, he was worried he'd do something to make her run.

"Thanks, Nash."

"You're welcome, baby. Do you want to come inside?"

"Yes."

Cree's heart flipped with hope. There'd been no hesitation in her answer whatsoever. He glanced at Wilder and then Nash and saw they were both happy about this change of heart, too.

Were they about to have all their dreams come true?

He fucking hoped so.

Nash wrapped an arm around Violet's shoulders and guided her toward the house.

Cree and Wilder exchanged glances as they followed them inside.

Once Nash had her seated on the sofa, Cree walked closer. "Do you want something to drink, honey?"

"No, thanks."

He frowned and glanced at Wilder again. His brother was looking just as uncertain as he felt. If she didn't want a drink, then why had she accepted their invitation to come inside? Maybe she wanted to ask if they'd heard anything about Luke's and Damon's investigation. That made sense to him.

"Did Luke or Damon bring over the statement for you to sign?" Wilder asked.

"Luke did. He also told me he contacted the Minneapolis Internal Affairs Division. Someone is investigating the Bemidji Sheriff's Department."

"That's good news, honey." Cree didn't have the heart to tell her Luke and Damon had already filled them in. Apparently, there had been a lot of complaints about the Bemidji sheriff and his deputies. He just hoped that IA were able to nail the asshole who'd ignored the plea for help from a fifteen-year-old girl.

"What's on your mind, sweetness?" Wilder asked.

"Um, uh. I want…"

Cree shifted so he could see her eyes and then clasped her hand. He realized she was nervous when he felt how cold her fingers were and her hand was trembling slightly.

"Why are you scared, honey? You know we wouldn't hurt you, don't you? What's wrong?"

"Nothing's wrong."

Cree knew something was going on, but he and his brothers couldn't help Violet until she told them what was up.

"We're men, baby," Nash said as he sat beside her and clasped her other hand. "Sometimes you have to hit us on the head with a two-by-four. Just spit it out, Violet."

She licked her lips nervously, swallowed audibly, and then drew in a deep, ragged breath. "I want to try a relationship with you."

Chapter Nine

Had she really just blurted that out?

Violet kept her gaze on the floor and waited with bated breath for a response. The air was rife with tension. She began to feel really uncomfortable and stupid when Wilder, Cree, and Nash remained silent.

Had they changed their minds? Was she too late?

Tears burned the back of her eyes, but she wasn't about to make more of a fool of herself than she had already. She blinked and forced them away.

Cree released her hand, and she held her breath as she waited for the inevitable rejection.

He cupped her cheek and then shifted her gaze up to his. The air exploded from her lungs when she met his heated green-eyed gaze and then his mouth was on hers.

She moaned and turned toward him as he licked over the seam of her lips.

Just as she opened to him, he drew back. Violet wanted to tell him to come back, but she bit her lip instead.

"Be sure that this is really what you want, honey."

She frowned and then glanced at Wilder when he perched on the coffee table across from her.

"If we start this, that's it, honey."

What does that mean?

"What my idiot brothers are trying to say," Nash said as he squeezed the hand he was still holding, "is that if we make love with you, from then on you'll be ours. Do you understand?"

"I'm not sure that I do," Violet stated coolly. "I'm don't go jumping from one man's bed to another."

"Fuck!" Cree spat.

"Shit, baby, that's not what I meant at all." Nash glanced at Wilder a little helplessly.

"What we mean is that when we make love to you, from then on you'll be ours. We want it all with you, Violet. We want you living in our home. We want the figurative picket fence and the two point five kids." Wilder locked gazes with her.

"We want the long haul, baby," Nash said.

"We want something that is going to last for the rest of our lives," Cree said. "So if you don't want that, you'd better say so now."

Relief surged through her blood releasing the tension in her taut muscles. She met each of their eyes and said, "I want that, too. I can't promise that this will work. I've never been in a relationship before and don't know how to deal with one man let alone three, but I'm willing to give this a try."

"That's all we can ask, honey." Cree brought her hand to his mouth and kissed the back of it.

"What time do you work tomorrow, sweetness?" Wilder asked.

"I start at one."

"That's perfect." Nash smiled.

She had no idea what he was talking about, but she smiled back. The smile slowly slid from his face and his pupils dilated as he stared at her. He grasped her waist and then lifted her into his lap.

Violet looped an arm around his neck and then she leaned up as he tugged her down and kissed her.

She'd only ever been kissed once before and that was by Wilder. Although she felt out of her depth, having Nash's lips on hers was heaven. She gasped when he nipped her lower lip and then groaned when he slid his tongue in along hers and then twirled it around.

Violet's breasts grew heavy, her areolae ruched, and her nipples grew hard. Her clit began to throb and her pussy grew damp and achy.

She loved how Nash tasted, all spicy, masculine, and sexy. He tasted different than Wilder but no less delicious and she couldn't wait to find out what Cree tasted like. He'd kissed her earlier but nothing like this. The kiss she and Cree had shared had been chaste in comparison.

And then she remembered she hadn't told them about her genetic condition.

She broke the kiss and gasped air into her starving lungs. "There's something I need to tell you all."

Wilder reached over and held her hand. "What is it, sweetness?"

"I have a genetic condition."

"Is it life-threatening?" Cree frowned.

"No."

"Thank fuck!" Nash hugged her waist. "You had us worried there for a moment, baby."

"Sorry."

"Tell us, Violet."

"I know you've probably noticed the strange color of my eyes, but what you may not know is that my pale skin, hair, and eye color are because of a genetic condition called Alexandria's Genesis."

"This condition doesn't affect your health does it, honey?" Cree asked.

"No. I'm perfectly healthy."

"Then what's the problem, sweetness?"

"Um, well, because of my genetics I'm not able to grow hair on my body other than my head, eyelashes, and eyebrows."

"Nowhere else?" Nash asked hoarsely.

"Uh. If I remember correctly I still have nose hair like everyone else. I never tan. If I get too much sun I turn pink or red and then just go back to my normal white."

"I love your skin, baby." Nash stroked a finger down her cheek. "It's so fucking soft."

"So you don't mind?" Violet asked.

"Why would we?" Wilder asked.

"Because I'm not like everyone else."

"We love that you're different, honey," Cree said sincerely. "Your differences are sexy and that's what attracted us to you first, but the more we got to know you, the more we realized you were definitely the woman we've been waiting for."

"So you won't be turned off by..." Her hand fluttered at her throat with embarrassment.

"Don't you know that most adult women would love to have naturally bare legs and pussy? Can you imagine how much money they're spending on getting waxed all the time?"

Violet smiled. She hadn't even thought of that.

Wilder stood and then helped her to her feet. She had to crane her neck to meet his gaze, and when she saw the hunger in his green eyes, she gasped.

"I can't wait to lick that bare pussy, sweetness. I know you are going to taste so good."

"Oh god."

"It's Wilder, sweetness."

He didn't give her a chance to respond, but swooped her up into his arms as he slanted his mouth over hers.

* * * *

Wilder wanted to shout with elation, but he was too busy kissing his woman. She'd finally agreed to have a relationship with him, Nash, and Cree. She was going to be theirs for the rest of their lives.

He couldn't wait to make love with her, to solidify their claim on her. His cock was so fucking hard he was hurting, but he needed to keep his lust under control. As he devoured her mouth, he carried her down the hallway toward the bedrooms.

Each time her tongue danced with his, his cock jerked and throbbed even more. He loved the sighs, groans, and gasps she gave as he kissed her and couldn't wait to find out what she sounded like in the throes of orgasm.

He lifted his lips from hers, sucked air into his burning lungs, and nibbled on her neck. She whimpered, her hands clutching at his shirt, and she melted against him. When she gasped and drew back, he cursed under his breath. He still had his utility and gun belt around his hips. He'd probably hurt her when she'd pressed against him.

"I'm sorry, sweetness. Let me get rid of this." He quickly divested himself of the belt and then removed his shirt. He caught his brothers doing the same from the corner of his eye.

Violet licked her lips as she glanced from him to Cree to Nash and back again. His cock twitched and pulsed in his pants when her eyes glazed over and her breathing increased, letting him know that she liked what she saw.

He handed his things over to Nash and didn't have to tell his brother to make sure their weapons were secured in the safe when he left the room. Being retired Marines, they knew all about locking up guns.

Wilder breached the gap between him and Violet again and slanted his mouth over hers. Her small cool hands landed on his chest, and she moaned as she began to caress him. He was so hungry for her he wanted to rip her clothes off, literally, and sink himself in her warm, wet pussy until he was balls-deep, but he needed to make sure his woman was with him every step of the way.

He groaned when her tongue tangled with his, and then he pushed his hands up under the hem of her shirt. She whimpered when he smoothed his hands over the soft, warm skin of her sides, and when she arched her chest toward him, Wilder knew she was ready for more.

Keeping his caresses slow and gentle he worked his way up her body until his hands were on the outside of her breasts. After wrapping an arm around her waist and bringing their lower halves together, he cupped one of her satin-covered breasts with his hand.

She whimpered and gasped into his mouth as he kneaded her feminine globe, and when he squeezed her nipple between his finger and thumb, she cried out.

Wilder broke the kiss and pulled her shirt up and over her head. He growled when he eyed her perfect breasts spilling out of the top of their satiny confines and his mouth watered for a taste.

Cree moved around behind her, and as he removed her confined white locks from the hair tie and began to comb out her braid with his fingers, he licked and nibbled up and down her neck.

As he bent to lick over the top of her breasts, Nash went down on his knees at Violet's side.

Wilder met her gaze and flicked the front clasp of her bra. When he noticed her chest was no longer rising and falling rapidly, he realized she was holding her breath.

"Breathe, sweetness," he ordered in a raspy voice. "You have nothing to be worried about. You're fucking gorgeous."

"Sexy as sin," Nash said as he tugged the button on her trousers open.

"Look at these beautiful breasts," Cree said in a growly voice as he cupped Violet's now bare breasts. "So damn gorgeous."

"Oh," Violet gasped when Cree began to knead her soft flesh.

Wilder brushed the bra straps from her arms and then tugged it off before dropping it to the floor.

"Lift your foot, baby." Nash tapped on her right foot.

Wilder held her steady as his brother removed both of her shoes and socks and then he pulled her slacks down over her hips and off.

His heart was beating so fast in his chest he couldn't catch his breath, but it was no wonder when he had all of his dreams standing in front of him in only a pair of mauve satin panties. He licked his lips as his gaze wandered over her sexy-as-sin body. Her dusky rose-hued nipples hardened further under his intent gaze, and he slowly lowered his head.

Violet gasped when he laved the flat of his tongue over first one hard nipple and then the other. When he drew one of her nubs into his mouth and began to suckle on the tip, she moaned.

Cree was skimming one hand up and down her back while he cupped and molded her other breast, alternately squeezing her ass cheeks every now and then.

When Violet fell against him as her legs gave out, Wilder knew it was time to up the ante.

He nodded to Cree and Nash. Nash rose before stepping back, and when Cree moved aside, he swept her up into his arms, carried her to the bed, and lowered her into the middle of the mattress.

She was so fucking beautiful. Wilder could have stayed where he was, eying her sexy body over for a long time, but right now he wanted to make love to her more than he wanted to take his next breath.

He knelt at the end of the bed, caressing over her soft, smooth shins before traveling higher and higher. Violet closed her eyes and moaned when he began smoothing his hands up her inner thighs, getting higher and higher, until his fingertips brushed the edge of her panties.

"Wilder," she gasped and opened her passion-hazed eyes to meet his.

"What is it, sweetness?"

"I want…I need…"

"We know what you need, Violet. Just relax and feel, sweetness."

Cree and Nash got up on the mattress next to Violet after removing their uniform pants.

Violet glanced at each of his brothers in turn and gasped when she noticed they were only wearing boxers. She blinked when she glanced at their crotches and quickly squeezed her eyed closed after seeing their hard ridges outlined by the formfitting knit material.

"Lift your hips, Vi," Wilder commanded as he hooked his thumbs into the sides of her panties.

When she arched up, he tugged her undies down. He was the one gasping when his eyes locked onto her soft, smooth folds. Her labia were a healthy blushing hue and drops of cream glistened on her lower lips.

After throwing her panties to the side, he hooked his arms under her knees, lifted and spread her legs and then dove right in.

She groaned as he growled. He licked her from bottom to top, taking a moment to swirl his tongue over her engorged nub before lapping his way back down to her creamy well and dipping his tongue inside.

"Oh, oh," she gasped.

Wilder glanced up her body just in time to see Cree kiss her voraciously. Nash was plucking and pinching at one of her nipples while suckling on the other. Violet had her head tilted back and her eyes closed as she panted.

Each time he swirled his tongue over her clit, enticing her body to produce more cream, he quickly lowered down to lap up her sweet honey.

When she started rocking her hips, Wilder knew she was getting close to orgasm and rimmed her cunt with his finger.

As he dipped his finger into her tight, hot, wet entrance, he twirled his tongue over her pearl and then delved in further.

She was so fucking tight, he hoped that when it finally came time to make love with her, she would be able to take him without feeling any pain. Wilder set about sending her to the stars, hoping that making her come before he penetrated her would be enough to ease his way into her tight pussy.

There was no doubt whatsoever in his mind that Violet had never been with another man.

Possessiveness surged into his heart, and he started to slowly pump his finger in and out of her soaked pussy.

"Oh." Violet's legs trembled in his arms, and from the way she started writhing, she was right on the edge.

He increased the pace and depth of his pumping finger when he felt that distended spongy spot inside her, he twisted his finger and rubbed it as he sucked her clit into his mouth.

That was all it took.

Violet cried out as she hurtled over the edge. Her internal muscles clamped around his finger before releasing and clamping down again. Her whole body shook and shivered as she climaxed.

Cree and Nash continued to suck and lick at her nipples while Wilder kept pumping his finger in and out of her cunt, licking over her clit until the internal contractions began to wane and finally cease.

When she threaded her fingers into his hair and tugged, he lifted his head from her pussy and withdrew his digit from her entrance.

Cree and Nash released her nipples and caressed their hands over her body, gentling her down from her climactic high.

Wilder shoved to his shaking legs and quickly stripped from the rest of his clothes.

He needed to claim Violet. Right now!

Chapter Ten

"Oh. My…" Violet couldn't drag her gaze away from Wilder's long, thick, hard cock.

It was big, just like he was, and while she was nervous about having…*that* deep inside of her, she was also eager.

She couldn't believe how much pleasure she'd just experienced at the hands and mouths of Wilder, Cree, and Nash. And there was more to come. She wasn't sure she'd survive the rest, but she was going to give it a damn good try.

She glanced to her sides when Cree and Nash rolled away from her, and then she locked gazes with Wilder as he crawled up onto the end of the bed. He was hovering over her on all fours, and while she tried to keep her eyes on his, she couldn't stop herself from gazing down their bodies. His balls were hanging between his legs and his hard dick was jutting out from his body, pointing right at her. Without conscious thought, she reached down and caressed her finger over the tip of his cock and down the velvety, soft shaft. She snatched her hand back when his cock jerked and bobbed, and quickly lifted her gaze to his again.

"As much as I would love to have you exploring my body, sweetness, that'll have to wait for another time. I need you, Violet."

"I need you, too," she gasped out.

She groaned when Wilder lowered his body to hers and gasped when his chest pressed against her aching nipples.

With his upper weight braced on his elbows, he lowered his head and took her mouth. His tongue slid along and twirled around hers, and she moaned as he shared the taste of her pussy with her. She'd have thought to be turned off by such a deed but found the opposite was in fact true. It was carnal and sexy and dirty, and she wanted so much more.

Wilder broke the kiss and then sat back up between her splayed thighs. She took in the sexy sight of his hand wrapped around the base of his cock and shivered with need when he pumped his hand up and down his shaft a few times.

When he aligned the head of his cock with her drenched entrance she sucked in a deep breath and held it.

Cree and Nash moved closer to her side and Nash cupped her cheek, turning her gaze toward his. "Don't hold your breath, baby, and don't tense up. Try and stay nice and relaxed for Wilder."

"Okay," she gasped out when Wilder pressed the broad bulbous head of his cock into her pussy.

"Fuck!" Wilder said in a growly voice. "You're so fucking wet. Hot and tight."

She would have agreed with him if she'd have been able to speak, but right now she couldn't have said a word if she'd been paid a million bucks. Wilder was so thick there was a slight burning sensation as her tissues stretched.

"You okay, honey?" Cree asked as he cupped a breast and then strummed his thumb over the tip.

"Yes!" Violet gasped and arched her chest up into Cree's hand and then bowed her hips up toward Wilder.

"Stay still, sweetness." Wilder clasped a hip to hold her down and then delved in a little deeper.

The nerves inside her pussy were so close to the surface they lit up with pleasure as he slowly worked his cock up inside her sheath. She could literally feel her muscles and channel stretching to accommodate his pleasurable intrusion. Liquid desire pooled in her belly. Her womb and sheath contracted as if trying to suck his cock in deeper, and she spread legs wider, hoping he'd take the hint and fill her to capacity.

"More!" Violet grabbed hold of his biceps and wasn't surprised when her hands looked so small against his huge, bulging muscles. Nor that her skin looked ghostly in contrast to his bronzed-tanned skin.

"I'll give you more, Vi. Just let me—" Wilder groaned when he pussy muscles rippled around his length as cream dripped from her pussy. "Fuck! Do that again, sweetness."

Violet squeezed her internal muscles around his hard dick, and when she loosened them again, Wilder sank into her until she could feel the tip of his cock nudging against her cervix.

"Oh." She shivered as goose bumps raced over every inch of her skin.

"Do you like that, honey?" Cree asked. "Do you like having Wilder's cock deep inside your pretty little cunt?"

"Oh. Yes!"

Wilder glanced toward Cree and Nash and nodded at his brothers. As they rolled away from her again, he blanketed her body, shoved a hand under her ass, and tilted her hips up toward his. He bent his head toward her and then kissed her rapaciously.

Violet clutched at his shoulders as he began to move.

He pumped his hips, gliding his cock in and out of her pussy with a slow gentle rhythm. Violet couldn't believe how amazingly good it felt to have Wilder making love with her. Already the tension and fire began to build, and though she wanted to experience the ecstasy of climax again, she also wanted this monumentally special moment to last forever.

When he released her lips, he licked his way over to her neck and sucked on the sensitive skin just beneath her ear. She moaned and groaned as she wrapped her arms around his neck and held on tight. He growled in her ear, before nipping at her lobe and then sucking it into his mouth, his warm breath in her ear sending tendrils of desire racing through her body.

"You feel so fucking good, Vi. I can't wait for you to come all over my cock."

Vi shuddered and hooked her legs around his hips, her heels digging into his ass. Being able to feel his buttocks flexing as he pumped his cock in and out of her pussy enhanced her need to a higher level.

He shifted his weight up onto his elbows and said, "Look at me, sweetness."

Violet opened her eyes and gazed up into his heated green eyes.

"You okay?"

She licked her lips and nodded. When he shifted on his knees and drove back into her, she cried out. As he'd glided back into her pussy, his shaft had rubbed over her clit, making her insides light up even more.

He pulled back and she gasped as she felt every ridge and vein as his thick cock caressed all those sensitive nerves inside her pussy.

And then he was kissing her again.

This time when he surged into her cunt, he went faster, deeper, and harder.

Her cry of pleasure was muffled against his mouth and it took her a few moments to realize she was digging her nails into his skin. She eased her grip on him and hoped she hadn't hurt him, but all thought fled when he began to rock into her faster, still.

No matter how much she panted for breath she couldn't fill her burning lungs and turned her head so she could gulp in air. She wasn't the only one breathing heavily. Wilder's breath sounded loud next to her ear, but she liked knowing she wasn't the only affected by their lovemaking.

Wilder was pistoning in and out fast and deep. Every time his cock drove into her pussy, he created a fiery friction that grew hotter and brighter.

The pressure inside grew, her muscles tautened and the liquid desire pooling in her belly began to spread throughout her body until she was shaking. Each time he delved into her wet pussy the pleasure got more intense. So much so that she wasn't sure she would survive it.

And then she was hovering right on the precipice.

All of a sudden Wilder shifted back up onto his knees. He tightened his grip on her hips, lifting her ass from the mattress, and then he was shoving down into her pussy in a fast, hard rhythm.

Violet toppled over the rim, screaming.

Her whole body shook and shivered as her pussy clenched around his shuttling cock only to loosen and clamp down again. She sucked air into her lungs and moaned as nirvana continued to wash over her. Each time Wilder pressed in deep sent another round of euphoria coursing through her vagina and body.

And then his rhythm faltered. She forced her heavy lids up and stared into his blazing green eyes. The veins and muscles in his neck were pulled tight, and if she hadn't known better, Violet would have thought he was in pain.

He withdrew from her pussy again, and as he stroked back in he made a low growly sound which continued as he drew back once more. When he surged forth this time, he yelled and froze deep inside of her.

Her pussy twitched with aftershocks as he emptied his cum deep inside of her body. She felt every twitch and jerk as he filled her with his seed and her pussy clenched in response as he ground his hips into hers. Finally, Wilder collapsed down onto her, his harsh breathing once again loud in her ears, but Violet didn't care.

Their lovemaking had been amazing, but this moment was more profound than the physical act. She was as close to a person as she'd ever been, but it wasn't only her body that was warm. Her heart and soul warmed, melting the ice she hadn't known that was entrenched in the organ. Violet was connected to Wilder on an emotional level, and it was the most amazing feeling. The only thing that could make her feel more, was to be as connected with Cree and Nash the way she was with their brother.

She couldn't wait to make love with them, too.

* * * *

Cree had kept a close eye on Violet while Wilder had made love to and claimed her. He'd been ready to step in and tell his brother to ease off if he'd seen discomfort or pain on Violet's face, but thankfully she'd been with Wilder every step of the way.

Although he wanted, no, *needed* to make love with and claim her himself, he wasn't about to interrupt Violet's and Wilder's bonding time.

He glanced over at Nash to see his brother was smiling. Cree grinned back and then returned his gaze to Violet when Wilder rolled them both to their sides. He and Cree had moved to the end and sides of the bed to give his brother room to make love with their woman. He loved hearing all the sounds of pleasure she made and hoped that she made the same sounds when it was his turn to claim her. While he hoped his turn would be soon, he wasn't about to pressure her. If she was too tired or sore, he and Nash would need to give her time to rest and recuperate.

Wilder kissed her softly on the lips, withdrew his arms from around her body, and rolled off the mattress. Violet sighed contentedly and then curled into the fetal position as she closed her eyes.

Cree nodded to Nash, and they both crawled back up the bed to lie on either side of her. Cree brushed a few strands of hair off her cheek. "Are you okay, honey?"

She opened her eyes and smiled at him. There was so much emotion in those amazing unusual orbs, his heart flipped in his chest and his breath hitched in his throat.

"I feel wonderful."

Cree winked at her and shifted closer until he was face to face with her. He kept his gaze locked with hers even when he heard Wilder come back from the bathroom.

"I've never felt anything so…" She shrugged as if she couldn't think of what she wanted to say.

"Orgasmic?" Nash suggested from behind her.

Violet nodded.

"Amazing?" Cree asked.

Violet nodded again. "So special."

Cree leaned forward and kissed her on the lips. She moaned and closed her eyes. Cree gazed at Nash when he nudged his shoulder, not breaking the kiss with Vi, and he took the damp cloth Nash handed him. He hadn't seen Wilder pass the cloth to his brother, but that was the only way he could have given it to him.

He dropped the cloth onto his hip, skimmed a hand up over Violet's thigh, and caressed back down to her knee. He gripped her leg and then lifted it up over his hip and tugged the cloth out from under her leg. She gasped when he wiped her folds clean and lifted her mouth from his.

"What are you…I can do that." A rosy hue crept up her face starting at her chest, and when she clasped his wrist, Nash grasped hers.

"I want to take care of you, honey." Cree tossed the cloth to the floor, wrapped his arm around her waist, and tugged her closer. He rolled to his back, taking Violet with him until she was lying on top of him.

Nash shoved up and then knee-crawled down the bed. Cree gripped her waist and lifted her further up his body until she was on her knees, straddling his hips. He clasped her wrists in his hands and brought her hands to his chest.

She shifted on her knees and moaned when his boxer-covered cock pressed against her bare pussy. Bracing her weight on her hands and knees, she rose up over him and looked down at his crotch. "Take them off," she ordered so softly he almost didn't hear her.

Cree hooked his thumbs into the waistband of his boxer shorts and shoved them down his hips and thighs, until they were around his shins. Making sure Nash wasn't in his way, he kicked them all the way off.

"Come here, honey," Cree said as he clasped her hips in his hands again. She nodded and lowered down onto him again, causing them to both moan when her pussy pressed against his hot, hard, aching cock.

Cree spread his legs further so Nash could get closer to Violet from behind, and then he cupped the back of her neck and pulled her mouth down to his. She gasped into his mouth and then began rocking over his dick. He groaned as her warm honey bathed his dick in her juices.

His balls felt harder than stones, and his cock pulsed and pre-cum bubbled up to the tip, he knew he couldn't wait any longer.

He tightened his hands on her hips and lifted her up as he kissed her hungrily. When her entrance kissed against the head of his erection, he arched his hips up and pressed into her.

She moaned and broke the kiss as she gasped in air, and when she leaned forward again, he waited for her kiss. Instead she tensed and then shoved down onto his cock hard and fast.

Cree growled deep in his throat as he threaded his fingers into her hair and brought her gaze back to his. "Are you okay? Did you hurt yourself, honey?"

"No." She sucked in another breath and then slowly lifted from his hard cock until just the tip rested inside her hot, tight, wet cunt.

"You feel amazing, Vi."

"So do you." She huffed out a breath and smiled at him as she sank down over him again.

Cree glanced up at Nash and nodded.

His brother nodded back, and then he shifted his arms around Violet and cupped her breasts in his hands as he licked and nibbled at the side of her neck.

Violet moaned and seemed to get lost in the sensations Nash was creating in her body, because she closed her eyes and stopped moving altogether.

Cree clasped her hips in his hands and lifted her up until he was just resting inside her humid entrance. He was the one moaning when she flexed around the tip of his dick. He took in her stunning face and the flush that tinted her creamy white skin a pink hue, and when the base of his spine began to tingle, he gritted his teeth. There was no fucking way he was going to come before his woman.

He glanced at Nash a little desperately when she sank back down over his dick, enveloping the hard, sensitive flesh with her tight, wet cunt as he tugged her down against his chest.

Cree threaded his fingers into the hair at the back of her neck and nudged her face up to his. He slanted his mouth over hers, pushing his tongue into her mouth and swirling it around hers. She whimpered as she drew air in through her nose, and while he kissed her voraciously, he caressed his free hand up and down her back. When she jolted, he skimmed his hand down to her hip again.

"Oh," Violet groaned and shook with need after breaking their kiss. She turned to gaze at Nash over her shoulder. "Wh-what are you doing?"

"I'm just trying to make you feel good, baby. Don't you like me playing with your ass?"

"Uh."

Cree tipped her gaze back to his, trying to read her expression. He nearly sighed with relief when he didn't find any fear in those amazing indigo-colored eyes.

Nash must have caressed over her star again, because she shuddered and her pussy rippled around him and she coated his cock in her sweet honey. Cree had to close his eyes and try to think of something mundane as he got a little closer to climax, but not a damn thing came to mind except for how wonderful it felt to be buried deep inside of Violet.

"It's…different. I never thought about…"

Cree leaned up and kissed her softly on the lips. "This is all about you, honey. With a ménage, we're all going to want to take you together eventually, but if you don't like it, all you have to do is say the word. All right?"

"So if I say stop, you'll stop?"

"Absolutely," Cree and Nash answered at the same time.

"You have all the control, Vi," Nash reiterated.

"Okay then." Violet sighed and was about to close her eyes, but Cree needed to make sure she was on board with what was happening even though she'd already answered the question with her body. "Answer the question, honey. Do you like Nash playing with your ass?"

"Yes," she moaned as Nash caressed over her star again. "I'd never thought…but it feels so good."

Nash leaned over and kissed between Violet's shoulder blades. "I think you're going to love it when we all make love to you together. Don't you, too, baby?"

"Oh." Violet trembled.

Nash rolled away from behind Violet and then stumbled toward the bathroom.

Violet frowned in his direction. "Where are you going?"

"I just need to get something. I'll be back in a second or two." Nash grinned and hurried into the adjoining bathroom.

"What's he doing?" Vi asked breathlessly.

Cree cupped her cheek and smoothed his thumb over her soft skin. He'd never get tired of touching his woman. He'd touch and kiss her all day long if she let him. "He's getting some personal lubrication, honey." He didn't give her a chance to ponder over that when he swooped in and started kissing her again. She kissed him as wildly and passionately as he was kissing her. His heart was so full of emotions that she had accepted to be in a relationship with him and his brothers. He was glad he had his eyes closed, because he was sure if they were open, Nash and Violet would have seen moisture welling.

He was so into Violet he wanted to tell her that he loved her, but he held back. If he started spouting those three words so early in their relationship, he was scared that she would think he was feeding her a line. If that was the case, then he had a feeling she would end their chance of wooing her there and then.

Violet lifted her mouth from his, panting heavily, and just as she met his gaze, Nash who'd climbed back on the bed did something that made her eyes widen. At first he thought his brother had hurt her, but when her lips parted more and her lids closed to half-mast, he knew the opposite was true.

Cree met Nash's gaze, and when he saw the smile on his brother's face, he relaxed again. He knew what Nash had done a second later because he could feel him pumping in and out of Violet's back entrance with his finger through the thin wall of tissues separating her pussy and anus. When she rippled and clenched around the length of his cock and his balls started to draw up closer to his body, he realized he was in trouble. "Move. Now!"

Nash smirked as he withdrew his finger from Violet's ass and then quickly moved out of the way.

Cree wrapped his arms around her and rolled until she was pinned under him. He groaned as she moaned when his cock pressed deeper into her vagina.

"Hold on to me, honey."

He lowered his chest until her nipples were brushing against his flesh, keeping most of his upper weight braced on his elbows so she could still inhale unhindered, and then he shoved a hand under her ass and tilted her hips up toward his.

Violet clutched at his shoulders, her breathing ragged as it sawed in and out of her lungs, but when she hooked her legs around his waist and squeezed him, Cree let loose.

He pulled back and then drove in hard, fast, and deep as he took her mouth with his.

She felt so fucking good, and while he was close, he wasn't about to lose total control.

Each time he withdrew he increased the pace of his pumping hips incrementally, and when he was buried balls-deep inside of her, he gave a slight twist to his hips, making sure to press against her engorged sensitive clit.

She dug her nails into his skin, moaning and groaning each time he advanced and retreated, and just when he felt the warning tingles move around to encompass his balls and the base of his cock, her internal walls clenched around his dick. They were both one stroke away from climaxing.

Cree released her mouth, shifted his hand until the tip of his finger had breached her ass, and then he drove into her again.

"Cree!" Violet cried as she started to come.

Cree growled long and low as he stroked into her contracting pussy twice more and then roared as fire shot up his dick. Lightning flashed before his eyes as his cock thickened more than it ever had and then he was coming so hard he saw stars.

His balls had nearly crawled up inside of his body, and he swore he could feel semen roiling around in his testes as they armed over and over again. The climax was the strongest, most profound experience of his life. By the time he'd spumed every drop of seed deep into Violet's pussy and womb, he was shaking and totally wrung out.

Cree blinked and tried to clear his vision, and when he glanced down at Violet, his spent, softening cock twitched. She was so fucking sexy and the most beautiful woman he'd ever set eyes on— and it had nothing to do with how gorgeous she was.

Violet Evans was the love of his life, and he would do anything and everything he could to keep her by his side.

Cree just hoped she felt half as much as he felt for her.

As he rolled them to their sides the hair on his nape stood on end, but he quickly pushed the disconcerting feeling aside. Right now, he needed to make sure Vi was eased down from such an amazing high.

However, no matter how hard he tried to push the alarming niggle aside, it wouldn't be budged. His intuition was telling him something was seriously wrong or something bad was going to happen.

He just hoped that it was to do with their new deputy positions and had nothing to do with Violet.

If something happened to her…Cree mentally shook his head. Nothing was going to happen to Violet. Not on their watch.

Chapter Eleven

"There's white water rafting and a lot of hiking tracks," the old man said. "If you decide to go hiking make sure you let someone know which track you'll be taking and how long you'll be gone. We don't want the local law out looking for someone who isn't missing."

Virgil nodded his head and smiled, tuning the old man out. He wasn't going to do any of the things the old-timer was telling him about, but he needed to keep up his appearance of being a tourist. He took the brochures, thanked the man for the information, and headed out.

He'd had been walking around the town of Slick Rock all day long, and while he'd had a few curious looks, he'd just smiled and ignored the locals' curiosity. He could play tourist just like anyone else. He'd made sure to stop in at the camping and fishing supply store at the western end of the main street, and he'd even gone to the tourist information window at the back of the store to get some pamphlets so that he looked as if he was interested in the things to do and see in the area.

The old guy at the information window had droned on and on, until Virgil had tuned him out but not because the old codger wasn't passionate about what he was doing or because he was boring—it was just that he'd had no interest in what he'd been saying. Although he'd made sure to nod and smile and make the appropriate noises in the right places, he had a feeling he hadn't fooled the old man at all. However, he didn't give a shit about what the old man thought about him.

Once he left the recreation goods store, he wandered over to sit on the bench in the park situated in the middle of the town and studied the map. Thankfully, it was current and even had the new housing estates on it.

As he breathed in the warm, fresh summer air, he tried to figure out how he was going to get his hands on the slut.

He'd been into the diner, making sure to wear his cap trying to hide his face in the shadows, but luckily, the bitch hadn't been anywhere in sight. As he stared at the map he brought the faces of the diner employees to the forefront of his mind. They'd all been women and while those sluts looked as if they were all in their early to mid-twenties, there was one that looked as if she was still in her teens.

Virgil had a feeling it would be much easier to target the teenager than any of the other women. Since they all worked together and Lilac was one of the owners, surely the girl would have her boss's contact information in her cell phone.

He smiled as the plan began to form in his mind. It might take him a few days so he could watch the teenager to learn her routine, but he was willing to take as much time as he needed to get what he wanted.

Lilac was the only woman he hadn't been with, and that pissed him off. He'd tried to get her out of his mind, but the craving to have her had never gone away. In fact, the obsession for the bitch had only gotten stronger until he felt as if he was going out of his mind.

There was no way he was leaving this small hick town until he had Lilac where he wanted her. Maybe he'd get a taste of the young girl first. He licked his lips in anticipation.

When he glanced around the park and noticed a couple of women watching him, Virgil decided he'd need to do some of the tourist things so he wouldn't look so suspicious.

He stood and hurried toward his car. Today he was going to go for a hike to bide his time. He remembered the teenager had worked all day on the weekends, but since she looked young enough to still be attending school, he would wait until late afternoon to go to the diner.

He was going to have to be careful in case Lilac was working, but since it had been ten years since her escape, he didn't think she'd recognize him. He'd changed from the skinny kid he used to be. He'd bulked up as well as grown a few more inches. There was no reason for her to suspect he was looking for her either, so hopefully, she wouldn't be on guard. The fact that he also shaved his head, which changed his whole appearance, was another plus.

He chuckled as he got into his car and started the ignition. This was going to be easier than he'd suspected. He'd use the girl to lure Lilac to him, and then he'd have two women in his clutches. Maybe he could have his cake and eat it, *two*.

He laughed at his own joke and headed out of town to one of the easier walking tracks.

As he drove, he thought about all the fun he was going to have.

* * * *

Nash got onto the bed just as Cree rolled to his feet. He'd had a hell of a time keeping his distance and allowing his brother time to kiss cuddle and stroke Violet back down from her climax, and while he wanted to make love with her and claim her more than he wanted to take his next breath, he wasn't going to push her. She'd already made love to Wilder and now Cree, and since she'd been a virgin, she had to be feeling more than a little tender.

He'd just settled onto his side on the mattress behind her when she rolled over so they were face to face.

"How are you feeling, baby?"

"Overwhelmed, wonderful, nervous, and satiated."

Nash frowned. "Why overwhelmed?"

"There are three of you, Nash."

"And?"

"I'm not used to any of this. It's a bit...scary."

"What are you afraid of, baby? Are you scared we'll hurt you?"

"Not physically, no."

Nash sucked in a steadying breath and cupped her cheek in his hand, stroking his thumb over her warm, soft skin. "I can promise you here and now that me and my brothers would never do or say anything to deliberately hurt you."

She licked her lips as she nodded. "I know that deep in my heart, but after what I saw and experienced growing up, it's hard to get it through my thick head."

"That's understandable, Vi. I know it's scary to put your heart out there and trust blindly, but I thought we'd already shown you we care for you. We wouldn't be here now if we didn't. I'd rather cut out my own heart than do anything to deliberately or even unintentionally piss you off and hurt you, baby. However, I'm...*we're* still human and are bound to make mistakes."

She blinked quickly when tears welled in her eyes. "I know. It's just that...there are three of you."

"Why does that matter?"

"What if I do something that annoys you, Cree, or Wilder? Will you want to call it quits?"

"No, baby, never. No one's perfect. As human's we all fuck up from time to time. We aren't naïve enough to think that everything will be smooth sailing. We care for you, Violet. I care for you so much already. If we get mad at each other, that doesn't mean we're going to walk away, and I'm hoping the same goes for you. It takes work to keep a relationship going, but as long as there is trust and love, as well as communication, we'll be fine."

She frowned for a moment and then smiled as she traced his lower lip with her finger. "How did you get so smart?"

"I'm not smart, baby. I'm just the average clueless male."

She smiled and shook her head. "You're all far from clueless. I'm the clueless one. I have no idea how a relationship works."

"All you need to do is follow your heart, baby. Just like we are." Nash hoped that she could see his heart in his eyes and guessed she had when she sucked in a deep breath.

"Will you please make love with me, Nash? I want to feel as connected to you as I do Wilder and Cree."

"I want that, too, baby. So much."

Nash pressed his lips to hers and groaned when she licked over his lips as she wrapped her arms around his neck. He opened his mouth and growled when she pushed her tongue into his mouth. He let her lead as long as he could before he took over. The kiss turned hot, wild, and carnal, and he didn't even realize he'd rolled them over until he broke the kiss to draw air into his burning lungs. She was lying on her back, her long white-blonde hair was in a messy halo around her head and shoulders, and her cheeks were once more heightened with desirous color.

She blinked her eyes open and then smiled up at him. Her usual lilac eyes had deepened to an indigo hue with her desire and her pupils were dilated. If he hadn't been so famished for her he would have spent hour upon hour kissing and caressing every inch of her sexy body. He wanted to lick her to orgasm, but his cock was throbbing along with each beat of his heart and he had a feeling it wouldn't take much for him to explode.

Nash lowered his head to her chest, licking and nibbling his way down to her gorgeous boobs. When he laved the flat of his tongue over one hardened peak, she whimpered. He shifted to the other side and circled her areola with the tip of his tongue, delighting in her sighs and moans as the velvety soft, rose-hued skin crinkled as it contracted.

When she arched her chest up toward his mouth, he didn't waste any time teasing her. Because he was so hot for her, he was worried he wouldn't be able to get her off before he came. However, since there was no way he was going to let that happen, he concentrated on feeding her fire.

Nash drew her nipple in his mouth and suckled on it firmly while he squeezed the other one between his finger and thumb. Violet gasped and groaned. He switched to the other nipple again and growled in approval when she began to rock her hips against his. His cock twitched and pulsed as pre-cum leaked from the tip.

He shifted up onto his knees between her splayed thighs and kept his gaze locked with hers as he caressed up and down her folds. She gasped and shuddered when he swirled his finger around her clit before dipping into her creamy, wet entrance.

"Nash, please?"

"Please what, baby?"

"Please make me yours."

"Roll onto your stomach, Vi," Nash ordered.

She frowned at him, but then rolled over.

He gripped her hips and pulled her up onto her hands and knees. "I want this to be good for you, baby, but I'm so triggered this is going to be hard and fast."

"Yes!" Violet sobbed her answer. "It's crazy. I want you so bad, Nash. It doesn't seem to matter that I've already come goodness knows how many times."

Nash's heart flipped and his breathing hitched. Excited hope filled his chest. Violet might not know it yet, but her words just confirmed that she had strong feelings for him and his brothers. She was just as hungry for him even after having several orgasms.

He took a deep breath and let it out slowly as he tried to get his raging need under control. He wrapped his hand around the base of his hard cock and aligned it with her pussy. After sucking in another breath, he began to press in.

Nash closed his eyes as her wet heat enveloped the head of his dick. She was so fucking hot and wet, and even though he was just inside of her, he could feel her clenching around him already.

"More," Vi demanded as she lowered her chest toward the bed.

He groaned when she pressed her hips back toward his and he clasped her hip.

"Stop, baby. Let me do all the work," he panted out between shallow breaths. "I don't want to hurt you."

"You won't hurt me, Nash. Stop holding back. Give me all of you."

The desperation in her voice threw Nash over the edge. He clasped her hips in his hands and slammed in deep. He paused to give her time to get used to having his cock inside of her body, but Violet was having none of that. She wiggled her ass against his groin and pubis, and spread her knees wider.

"Nash, if you don't fuck me, I'm gonna scream."

Nash chuckled to himself because with each word she'd spoken her voice had gotten louder and louder.

"Put your shoulders on the bed, baby."

He waited until she did as he'd ordered and then covered her back with his front as he began to pump his hips. His breathing increased and the tingles started at his lower back two strokes later. *Fuck*! Maybe he wasn't going to last after all.

* * * *

Violet had never experienced such an intense need in her life. She couldn't believe how hungry she was to have Nash make love to her after making love with Wilder and Cree one after the other. She should have been a boneless heap of flesh, but that was far from the case. Her pussy was a little tender, but not bad enough to stop her from making love with Nash, as well. She was so wet the insides of her upper thighs were coated with cream, and her pussy and womb were aching. Now that she knew what it was like to make love with Cree and Wilder, she wanted, needed to be with Nash, too.

The hunger was so intense she was nearly in tears, and if she'd been bigger and stronger, she would have shoved him onto his back, straddled his hips, and taken him inside of her before he could blink. And now that she'd had something in her ass, she craved to have that hole filled, too.

When Nash blanketed her back with his body, she wanted to shout for joy. Her internal muscles quivered around his long, thick cock, and juices leaked from her pussy.

Just as she was about to demand that he move, he mumbled something under his breath and pushed up to his knees again. She mentally bemoaned the loss of heat, but when he withdrew from her pussy and drove back in, all thought fled.

Nash had taken her at her word and was now surging in and out of her sheath hard, fast, and deep. The sound of their bodies slapping together was the only sound in the room other than their heavy breathing.

And then her breath froze in her lungs when he pressed a finger to her rosette and began to stroke into her back entrance.

"Oh," Violet moaned and shivered as the tension in her womb and vagina grew.

"You like that, baby?" Nash asked in a hoarse voice.

"Yes."

Nash made a growly sound as his other hand caressed from her hip, over her belly to the top of her mound. "You're going to love it when we all make love to you at the same time. Just imagine it, Vi. One of us will be fucking this sexy cunt." He paused as he slid his finger into her folds and caressed the tip lightly over her clit. "One of us will fuck this gorgeous ass." He stroked his finger in and out of her back entrance. "And one of us will fuck between those perfect pink lips."

Words were beyond Violet. She trembled as she envisaged Nash's words in her mind. The coil grew tauter each time he shuttled his hard cock in and out of her aching pussy. She was so turned on cream was dripping from her sheath like a leaking faucet. She cried out when he began to rub over her clit with firmer strokes. Violet felt out of control with need, and each time Nash shoved into her, the friction along her wet walls drove her closer and closer to the edge.

Air was sawing in and out of her lungs like a noisy bellow, and she clutched at the sheets as the pressure inside grew to astronomical proportions.

And then she could hear nothing but white noise and the rushing whoosh of her own blood racing past her eardrums.

Violet was hovering on the edge of a precipice with no way of knowing which was up, down, or sideways.

With the next beat of her heart, Violet was tossed into the tumultuous cataclysmic storm.

She screamed as nirvanic rapture washed over her, making her whole body quake. She shook and shivered as it felt as if her whole frame orgasmed. Her pussy clamped down hard around Nash's still pistoning cock over and over.

Streaks of lightning flashed before her eyes, or maybe it was stars streaking past as she flew up into the heavens.

Juices gushed from her sheath, dripping onto her inner thighs before trickling down her legs to her knees.

When her lungs began to burn and the bright lights began to fade, Violet realized she'd stopped breathing and gulped air into her oxygen-depleted organs. The blackness began to fade and as her awareness returned, she could hear Nash grunting each time he hammered his hips against her ass while he continued to drive his cock in and out of her pussy, and pumped his finger in and out of her ass.

Just as the internal contractions began to wane, Nash pinched her clit between his fingers, sending her straight back up to orgasmic heights.

Her mouth gaped open on a soundless cry, and this time there were no streaks of lights or lightening. Dark spots formed in front of her eyes, and she was so caught up in the cataclysmic pinnacle she had no idea if her eyes were open or closed.

Nash shoved into her once more, and his shout of completion seemed to come from a long way away. She tried to push the darkness in front of her eyes back, but it was a losing battle.

Her head swam with lightheadedness, and while her body was still shivering and shuddering with aftershocks, she was also highly sensitive to each pulsing contraction of Nash's cock as he filled her with his cum.

And then she sank into the mattress as the euphoria snatched into unconsciousness.

Chapter Twelve

Nash nuzzled his nose against Violet's neck. When she'd passed out just after she'd climaxed the night before, his heart had stopped beating. He'd been scared he'd hurt her while he'd been making love with her and had shouted for Wilder and Cree. They'd come bursting into the bedroom from the hallway, and it hadn't been till after he and his brothers made sure that Violet was all right that Cree had realized he'd been so wrapped making love with his woman, he hadn't even noticed that Cree had walked out of the en-suite bathroom after cleaning up and left the bedroom.

He and Wilder had slept the rest of the night with Violet between them, but she'd been so tired and worn out from their lovemaking, she'd barely stirred. Nash just hoped that they would get to spend all their nights with her snuggled between them, but with them all working the afternoon shift, he wasn't sure that was going to happen. However, he'd take what he could get.

When she sighed and stirred beside him, he leaned up onto his elbow and brushed the strands of hair away from her face. She smiled, sighed again, and blinked her eyes open. Wilder glanced at him before turning his gaze to Violet. His brother's gaze softened with love, and the smile that curved his lips was one that Nash had never seen before. He wondered if he looked as happy as Wilder, and guessed he did.

After serving in the Marines, Nash didn't think he'd ever feel anything ever again. He and his brothers had had to cut off their hearts so they could do their jobs while they were on tour. Some of the things he and his brothers had seen while they were in the military would have driven them insane if they hadn't learned to lock their hearts away, and while he sometimes wished he could block out some of those horrific memories, serving his country had made him the man he was today.

If he, Wilder, and Cree hadn't signed up they might not be where they were today and might never have moved to Slick Rock or met Violet. That would have been a travesty in his eyes. They could have missed ever meeting the one special woman that was the perfect fit for him and his brothers.

Violet was already the love of his life, and he wasn't sure he'd be able to handle it if something ever happened to her.

"Morning," Violet whispered.

Nash pushed his introspection aside and stroked a finger over Violet's small straight nose. "Hi, baby. Did you sleep well?"

"Yeah. I slept like a log."

"Do you have trouble sleeping often, sweetness?" Wilder asked.

She swallowed and nodded. "Most nights."

"You have nightmares?" Nash asked.

"Yes." She met his gaze. "I should have outgrown them, but I always end up dreaming about the horrible things those men and boys did to the women and other girls."

"I'm so fucking glad you escaped, baby."

"I am, too, but I've never stopped worrying about Rose and Fleur."

"You shouldn't feel guilty, Vi." Wilder slipped his arm beneath her neck and tugged her closer to his body.

"I should have done more." She blinked when tears pooled in her eyes. "I should have gone to other police stations, but I thought leaving a letter under the door to the Bemidji Sheriff's Department would have been enough."

"Had you ever met the sheriff or deputies?" Nash asked.

She shook her head. "No, but surely that shouldn't have mattered. Their job is to serve and protect, but as far as I know, they did nothing."

"Luke and Damon have been to Internal Affairs and told them what happened. They're currently being investigated," Wilder explained.

"I thought I heard voices." Cree smiled as he entered the room carrying a tray with four steaming mugs on it. "I brought you some coffee."

As soon as Cree set the tray on the bedside table near him, Nash picked up the cup with the cream in it, and after Wilder helped Violet into a sitting position with her back resting against the headboard, the sheet tucked over her breasts and under her arms, he handed her the mug of coffee.

"Thanks, Cree." She met his gaze and then took a sip of coffee. "Just the way I like it."

Nash passed Wilder his mug before picking up his own. Cree grabbed the remaining cup and then kneeled on the mattress near Violet's feet.

"Do you have any plans for the day?"

She shook her head after she swallowed a gulp of coffee. "Other than some laundry, no."

"Luke has invited us out to his ranch for a late BBQ lunch. Major, Rocco, Ace, and Delta will be there, as well," Wilder said. "We'd love it if you came with us."

"I don't want to intrude." Violet shook her head.

Nash was about to reply, but Cree tugged his cell phone from his pocket, swiped a finger across the screen, and then made the call. He put the speaker on so that they could all hear the conversation.

"What's up Cree?" Luke asked by way of greeting.

"Just wondering if we could bring Violet to the BBQ this afternoon?"

"Why the hell would you call to ask that? It was a given that you'd bring Violet since you're all dating her."

"We know that, but Violet said she didn't want to intrude. You're on speaker, by the way. Violet and my brothers can hear everything you say."

"Good," Luke said. "Violet, I expect you to be here between two and three with your guys. Okay?"

"Are you sure—"

"Don't argue, woman. Come out to the ranch and have some fun. Delta and her men are going to be here, too."

"Do you want me to bring something?" Violet asked.

"Just you and your men. Flick has everything under control."

"Okay. Thanks, Luke."

"You're welcome, honey. See you all this afternoon."

"See you then," Cree said before disconnecting the call.

Nash was happy to see the tension had eased from Violet's shoulders. She was always so intense and seemed worried about being an inconvenience. He and his brothers were going to have to work on that issue. Hopefully, she would gain more confidence as she spent more and more time with them, but his ultimate goal was having her fall in love with them.

He just hoped they succeeded in their plans.

* * * *

Virgil was driving down the main street of Slick Rock intent on getting to the white-water rafting venue, but when he saw the big truck coming toward him and caught sight of the woman in the passenger seat, his plans changed. Luckily, he was wearing his baseball cap and he ducked his head so she wouldn't be able to see his face, but she was too intent on whatever the driver was saying to take any notice of him or anyone else, for that matter. After checking his mirrors to make sure no one was behind him, he indicated and pulled toward the side of the road. He watched the truck in his rearview and side mirrors and when the vehicle disappeared from view, he made a U-turn.

Thankfully, he'd used a false name when he'd booked for his afternoon out and he'd been smart enough to pay cash. He didn't care about the money he was losing by not showing up. All he cared about was getting his hands on that bitch.

He made sure to stick to the speed limits so he didn't call any unwanted attention to himself and followed the truck at a distance. When it turned into a driveway leading to a ranch twenty minutes later, he didn't slow his car as he continued down the road.

When he found a safe place for another U-turn, he turned back and this time drove past the driveway entrance slowly. His heart slammed against his ribs when he spotted the sheriff's vehicle parked near the house. Virgil pressed his foot down on the accelerator and didn't breathe easy until he was back in town. His thoughts raced in turmoil for all of five minutes as he wondered why the slut was visiting the local law enforcement. It took another few minutes for logic to kick in.

Lilac and the other women who owned and worked at the diner probably interacted with the sheriffs and deputies of the town on a regular basis. Even he had to admit the food served at the greasy spoon was more like what would be found in a restaurant.

He sighed with relief but then growled with anger. He was still no closer to getting his hands on the slut. He'd decided to follow her and those bastards, hoping that they would lead him right to her front door. Now he was going to have to go back to his original plan of following the schoolgirl and snatching her. He just hoped it was going to be as easy as he thought it would be.

Now he knew what he was going to do he had to figure out how to implement his plan.

Hopefully, in a week or less, he would have Lilac Primrose right where she should have been ten years ago.

* * * *

Violet smiled shyly at the sheriffs and the others in greeting. Other than when she was working, she wasn't used to being around so many people and felt way out of her comfort zone. Wilder and Nash must have seen or felt how uncertain she was because they moved in until their arms were rubbing against her shoulders.

She gazed around the alfresco dining area, which was at the back of the house, and leaned in against Wilder. Nash clasped her hand in his and Wilder wrapped an arm around her shoulders.

"Are you okay, sweetness?" Wilder asked after he bent down to whisper in her ear.

She nodded and smiled as she stared into amazing green eyes. She'd never get sick of looking into Wilder's, Cree's, or Nash's eyes. Although they were mostly the same beautiful emerald green, there were subtle differences. Wilder's were nearly all green with a couple of flecks of gold. Cree's had a thin ring of blue on the outside edge of his irises, and Nash had a few flecks of the brown.

"Violet!"

She turned her gaze in time to see Delta barreling toward her. Her business partner was smiling, and there was a happy twinkle in her eyes. She had also gained more confidence about using her voice thanks to her fiancés, Major, Rocco, and Ace.

Violet stepped away from Wilder and Nash and hugged Delta back when the other woman wrapped her arms around her. Tears burned her eyes, but she blinked them away. For the first time in her life she had real friends, people she could talk to and rely on if she ever needed help, but that wasn't all. She had three wonderful, kind, loving men she could lean on and knew would have her back if she was ever in trouble.

Delta squeezed her harder and then stepped back. She was signing something to her but going way too fast for her to keep up. Major must have seen her dilemma because he chuckled and clasped his fiancée's shoulder to gain her attention, before he started signing to Delta. "Slow down, baby. Not everyone is as fast as you are at reading what you're saying." Major turned to Violet. "She was telling you how glad she is you're here."

"Thanks." Violet smiled as she signed back.

"Come and sit down everyone," Flick said loudly. "The food is ready."

Violet sat between Cree and Nash with Wilder on Cree's right.

"How are you all settling into Slick Rock?" Felicity asked. The other woman was smiling at her husbands as they made sure their children had food on their plates. Her heart filled with yearning as she watched the big, muscular sheriff with his daughter. The little girl couldn't have been much more than five years old, but from the looks of things she had her daddies wrapped around her little finger.

"I wish I'd found this town years ago," Violet finally answered and then cleared her throat when her emotions threatened to overwhelm her. "There are so many wonderful people living here."

Cree caressed a hand up and down her back, and when she turned to meet his gaze, she had to suck in a couple of deep breaths at what she saw in his eyes. She glanced at Nash to see him looking at her with the same expression, and when she noticed Wilder lean forward and wink at her, she nearly started crying. There was love in their gazes and it was all directed at her.

"You are so right, sister." Flick raised her wine glass. "I'd like to propose a toast." She waited while the women picked up their glasses and the men reached for their bottles of beer. "To friendship, family, and love."

"Here, here," everyone responded as they sipped their drinks.

The afternoon was one of the best Violet had ever had. With every sip of her wine she'd relaxed a little more and had ended up joining in conversations and laughing along with everyone else.

After the meal was over and the women had cleaned up, the men stripped off their T-shirts and played a game of tag football with the children. Violet had always imagined how a family and friends should play and laugh with each other, but this was the first time she'd ever seen that her dreams hadn't been just fantasies.

As the sun was setting and they said their goodbyes, Violet hoped that one day she would be able to return the favor of hosting a BBQ or meal at her house with her men by her side. She sighed happily as she leaned against Nash's shoulder as they headed back home.

* * * *

Virgil was hot, tired, hungry, and pissed. He'd spent the last three to four hours sitting in his stinking hot car waiting for that bitch and the assholes she was with to leave that ranch. The anger that was roiling inside of him got worse with each passing minute. When he got a hold of her he was going to make sure she paid for his discomfort.

The only consolation was that he was parked on the edge of town near the motel and he'd ducked back to his room a time or two to use the facilities and grab a few bottles of water so he didn't dehydrate. It had been a risky move since the fuckers could have driven past while he hadn't been in his car, but he had a feeling he hadn't missed them.

He'd made sure to move his rearview mirror and passenger driver's side mirror so he had a clear view of the road behind him and he'd slunk down in his seat to keep prying eyes from seeing him. Of course he had all four windows open and he'd parked under the shade of a tree, but it was hot enough to fry an egg on the hood of his vehicle and he was sweating up a storm. His clothes were soaked through with sweat, and he had the headache from hell.

He glanced in his mirrors when he heard a low rumbling coming from behind and when he saw the black truck coming toward him, all his pain and discomfort faded. His hours of boredom had been worth it after all. As the truck drove past he made note of the license plate and waited a minute or so before he sat up and started his car.

He followed the truck to the other side of town and into one of the new housing estates. He wanted to turn down the street the vehicle did but decided to bypass it instead when he saw that it was a cul-de-sac. However, now that he had a street he would come back in the early hours of the morning to scope things out. Maybe he'd be able to get to the slut without using the teenage bitch after all.

* * * *

Cree helped Violet from the truck and then guided her toward the house. Her eyes were heavy with tiredness but there was a lightness about her he'd never seen before. He and his brothers had barely been able to keep their gazes from her as she chatted and laughed happily with the other women. When Billy and Tom had suggested that all the men play a game of tag football with the kids, he'd wanted to refuse so he could keep watching his woman, but there was no way he could have disappointed those sweet little girls. They'd been so excited about their daddies' suggestion, they'd started clapping their hands as they jumped up and down.

"Tired, honey?" Cree asked as he led Violet to the sofa.

"Yeah, but it's a good tired."

Cree sat beside her and tugged her closer as he wrapped an arm around her waist. He glanced up at Wilder and wondered what the hell was going on with his oldest brother. Luke had pulled him to the side just before they'd left the ranch, and from the intent conversation and the anger in the sheriff's eyes, whatever he'd been saying wasn't good. Cree had seen Nash looking at them, too, but they hadn't wanted to bring Violet's attention to whatever was happening as they'd said their goodbyes. Wilder would no doubt fill them in on what was going on later tonight.

"Are you going to stay with us tonight, baby?" Nash asked as he sat on Violet's other side.

"If you're all okay with that."

Nash cupped her face between his hands and turned her gaze toward his. "We're okay with it, baby. You can stay here whenever you want."

Nash lowered his mouth to hers and kissed her passionately.

Chapter Thirteen

Violet moaned when Nash licked into her mouth. All afternoon she'd been trying to ignore the desire simmering in her body and blood. Now, there was no reason to hold back. She broke the kiss with Nash, scrambled up onto her knees, and then lifted a leg over his until she was straddling his hips. She sat on his strong, thick thighs and dropped to her ass.

Nash stared at her intently as he cupped her hips in his big hands, and when she saw the hunger in his eyes, a shiver of heat coursed up her spine. It was like a flip had been switched when she saw how turned on he was. Usually she liked to stay in the background, but with each minute she spent with Wilder, Cree, and Nash as well as the other people she was quickly becoming friends with, her confidence grew.

She needed them all so much she couldn't wait another minute and she became the aggressor.

Violet leaned forward, licked over Nash's lip, and then delved inside his mouth with her tongue. He growled as he moved one hand to thread into the hair at the back of her neck and the other hand on her hip tugged her closer. She gasped and then groaned when the hard ridge of his cock pressed up against her crotch and she began to rock her hips.

"Look at our woman," Wilder rasped out. "She's on fire."

"So fucking sexy," Cree groaned.

Violet wanted to yell at them to touch her, too, but since that would mean she'd have to stop kissing Nash, she didn't. When he stroked into her mouth with his tongue she tangled and glided her tongue with and along his before she started sucking on it.

Nash yanked gently on her hair breaking their kiss, and then he grasped her ass cheeks with both of his hands. "Wrap around me, baby."

Violet draped her arms around his neck and hooked her legs around his waist, and then squeaked when he rose, taking her with him. She didn't need to see to know that he was carrying her toward the bedroom, or that Wilder and Cree were right on their heels.

She licked at the yummy-tasting, slightly salty skin on his neck and then nipped his earlobe before sucking it into her mouth.

"Fuck! If you keep doing that, baby, it'll be over before we've even started." Nash squeezed both her cheeks, causing her to moan again.

She was so wet her undies were soaked through and maybe her shorts were, as well, but she didn't care. All she wanted in this moment was to be naked and making love to her men.

When Nash lowered her feet to the floor, she unhooked her legs and arms and wobbled back a step. She gazed at each of her men and shivered at the hunger in their eyes. Her pussy clenched and cream dripped onto her panties.

"Take your clothes off, sweetness," Wilder ordered as he ripped his T-shirt up and over his head before dropping it onto the floor.

Violet licked her lips as she stared at his wide shoulders and muscular pecs.

"Violet, if you don't want your clothes to be ruined, you better take them off. Now!" Wilder commanded.

She forced herself her arms to move so she could remove her clothes, but she kept her gaze moving between her men as they stripped off. She sucked in a breath when they kicked their shoes off and dropped their shorts and boxers before kicking them away.

Violet had removed everything except for her panties and was about to take them off, too, when her men pounced.

One minute she was staring at their delectably buff, tall, sexy bodies and the next she was lying completely naked flat on her back, her arms and legs splayed wide with Nash between her thighs.

"Oh," she moaned at the first lick of Nash's tongue up through her drenched folds.

"Hmm," Nash growled. "You taste so fucking sweet."

Wilder and Cree climbed onto the bed on either side of her. Cree cupped one breast and lowered his head to the other. Wilder palmed her cheek, turned her head toward him and slanted his mouth over hers.

She trembled as the need deep in her womb and pussy intensified until her whole body was quaking. She gasped air in through her nose as she tongue-dueled with Wilder. When Cree pinched and plucked at one nipple while scraping the edge of his teeth of the other, she arched her chest toward his mouth.

Her cry of pleasure when Nash began to flick the tip of his tongue over her clit while penetrating her with his finger was muffled by Wilder's kisses. Violet was so hungry for more, she didn't know if she could stand their blissful torment.

Cree released the nipple he was suckling on just as Wilder lifted his lips from hers. Wilder licked and nibbled down her chest and Cree grasped her chin before turning her gaze toward him. She only had time to draw in a breath and blink once before Cree was kissing her rapaciously.

Violet sobbed with pleasure as the pressure inside began to build, and while what they were doing to her was out of this world, she needed more.

She reached out toward Cree and caressed her hand over his bulging toned pectorals, down over his ripped abs, toward his groin. She sifted her fingers through his trimmed pubes, savoring the growl he breathed into her mouth, and then wrapped her hand around his cock. She pumped her hand up and down his erection a few times and then explored lower. When she felt the soft skin of his scrotum under her fingertips, she carefully moved her hand closer and cupped his sac. She rolled his testes gently in her hand, and when he groaned after breaking the kiss, she shook and creamed herself.

Wilder released her nipple and Nash gave her a pussy a last lick before he lifted his head to meet her gaze.

It was hard to focus when her vision was hazed over with desire, but she was able to clear her sight after blinking a couple of times.

"Why did you stop?" she asked after her breathing slowed a little.

"We're going to make love to you together, baby," Nash explained. "But we need to prepare you first."

"Oh," Violet moaned and shook as she climaxed.

"Fucking beautiful," Wilder growled just before he flipped her over onto her stomach.

Cree grabbed a pillow and shoved it under her hips.

"I need her ass higher," Nash said.

Cree tapped her shoulder. "On your hands and knees, honey."

Violet brought her knees up under her and then pushed up onto her hands.

"Good girl," Wilder praised just before he reached into the bedside drawer and pulled a tube of lube out, which he handed to Nash.

She shivered when she heard the top pop open and tried not to flinch when Nash pressed the tip of his cool, moist, lubed-covered finger onto her ass.

Since Violet had already experienced some anal play and had liked it, she didn't tense up when Nash caressed over her star. Nor when he penetrated her with first one finger and then the other. She moaned when he spread his fingers, stretching out her tight muscles, and gasped when he started thrusting them in and out of her ass.

She hadn't even noticed she'd lowered her head or closed her eyes, until Cree and Wilder both cupped a breast each. A whimper escaped from her parted lips when they began to knead the globes.

She groaned when Wilder thrummed one nipple with his thumb and Cree squeezed the other.

When Nash added another finger to her back entrance, she couldn't help but tense up. She didn't know how Wilder knew, but guessed Nash had indicated she was having trouble. He shifted on the mattress until his head was under her chest, and as he began to suck and lap on her nipple, he slipped his other hand between her legs.

Violet shivered as liquid heat pooled in her body, and the fire began to race through her blood as Wilder made light circles on her clit. Cree grasped a handful of her hair and turned her toward him. As soon as her lips were level with his, he slammed his mouth over hers.

Violet sobbed with pleasure as her body lit up like a search light.

When Nash had added a third finger to her ass, she hadn't been sure she could take anymore, but now that Wilder was caressing her clit and sucking on her nipple while Cree kissed her, the burning pinching pain was no more. Feel-good endorphins were coursing through her blood and all she could think about, all she wanted, was to have all three of her men inside of her body, making love to her simultaneously.

The coil inside her grew tauter, her blood grew hotter, and her need to make love with her men strengthened.

She pulled her mouth from Cree's, sucked in a lungful of air, and said, "Please?"

When Nash eased his fingers from her ass, she groaned with frustration.

"She's ready."

Violet must have blinked or was too caught up in her own hunger to be aware of what was happening, but when her mind finally engaged, she realized she was straddling Cree's hips and Nash was behind her.

Wilder was up on his knees right next to her, his cock practically in her face.

Just as she was about her wrap her hand around Wilder's erection, Cree lowered her down over his cock.

She groaned as his hard dick stretched her wet tissues wide, the sound blending with Cree's low growl.

Violet braced her hands on his chest and pushed down until his cock was embedded balls-deep in her pussy. Her internal muscles clenched and released as she got used to his pleasurable intrusion. Again, she turned toward Wilder, and just as she wrapped her hand around his shaft, Nash pressed the head of his penis against her star.

Cree covered her breasts with his hands, molding the globes before brushing his thumbs back and forth over her aching nipples.

"Lean forward a bit, baby," Nash ordered. "Don't worry about falling. Cree will hold you up."

Violet gulped in air as she leaned forward. She licked her dry lips as she stared a Wilder's cock. There was a drop of clear fluid glistening in the slit on the tip of his cock and she was salivating for a taste.

"You'll have a taste soon, sweetness, but Nash needs to get in that sexy ass first."

"Oh god," she moaned.

"Take a deep breath for me, baby. When I start pushing in, use those muscles inside and try to push me out as you exhale." Nash's warm, moist breath caressed her ear, causing her to shiver.

And then he was pushing inside of her.

Her eyes widened at the unbelievable pressure as the head of Nash's cock popped through the tight entrance, and she glanced desperately down at Cree. He gazed at Wilder and nodded. Wilder reached between her legs and twirled his finger over her wet, throbbing clit.

"Breathe, honey," Cree rasped out his command.

Violet exhaled and remembered to try and push Nash out with her muscles. His cock sank in another few inches. She panted heavily and tried to stop the instinctive clenching of her rear passage, but it was almost impossible to get control of a reflexive action.

Wilder removed his hand from her pussy just as Nash wrapped an arm around her waist. He caressed up and down her thigh and then over her folds before he began to finger her clit.

"You feel so fucking good, baby. So hot and tight. Are you all right? Am I hurting you? Do you need me to stop?"

Although Violet was a little uncomfortable with such a carnal, erotic act, she was no longer feeling any discomfort and didn't want Nash to stop. She couldn't believe how many sensitive nerves there were in her ass, nor the pleasure she was gaining even though Nash still wasn't in her back entrance all the way. She felt so full with Cree's cock shoved deep into her pussy and Nash's penetrating halfway into her rosette, but she wanted all of him. She wanted, *needed* to have all three of her men filling her at the same time. She was already connected to them on an emotional level, but Violet had a feeling once she had each of them inside of her, that connection would pale in comparison to what was to come.

"Use those muscles again, Vi," Nash said through his panting breaths.

Violet inhaled deeply, and as she exhaled she pushed back against Nash.

She whimpered as pleasure and pain warred in her nervous system, but again, the pleasure overrode the pain. And when she felt Nash's front pressed against her back, she wanted to shout with relief.

Instead she turned toward Wilder again.

He was waiting for her.

He bent over and kissed her passionately on the lips, and when he broke the kiss he wrapped his hand around the one she still had around his shaft and began to move her hand up and his hard cock.

"Just like that, sweetness. You hand feels amazing on my cock."

Now that she had Cree and Nash in her pussy and ass, feminine power surged through her body. She needed to know what Wilder's cock tasted like. She kept her gaze locked with his, tugged gently on his dick until he moved a little closer, and then she bent over and to the side.

Wilder gasped when she dipped the tip of her tongue in the small opening on the top of his cock, and when she swallowed his sweet-salty essence down, he stopped breathing.

She glanced up at him as she opened her mouth over his dick and sucked him in.

Wilder groaned as he combed his fingers into her hair, and then he was gripping the strands in his clenched fist.

Violet couldn't believe how wonderful he tasted and set about getting more of his juices as she started to slowly bob her head up and down over him. She didn't notice she'd stopped moving her hand until he gave it a gentle squeeze, just before he began caressing the rest of his cock with her hand.

Having Wilder's hand moving hers was so sexy, her internal muscles clenched, causing both Cree and Nash to moan and more juices to leak from her pussy.

"I can't stay still any longer," Nash gasped out. "She's so fucking tight and squeezing me so hard, I'm not gonna last."

"Me neither," Cree growled.

"Then let's make our woman come," Wilder panted.

Violet moaned as Nash withdrew from her ass, and when he stroked back in Cree glided out of her pussy. She swirled her tongue around Wilder's cock head, and when he jerked as it slid over a sweet spot just under the crown, she laved that spot with the flat of her tongue over and over.

"Violet," Wilder growled, as he tugged on her hair.

The slight pricks of pain on her scalp only seemed to ramp up her hunger more. She groaned as she slid her mouth back over Wilder's cock, taking him in further than before. When she felt his dick touch the back of her throat, she almost gagged and backed off. As she drew back, she suctioned in her cheeks, making her mouth as tight as she could and knew he loved what she was doing when he made a deep rumbling sound in his chest.

"Slow down, sweetness. You're going to make me come too fast."

Violet hummed in acknowledgment, but since that was the whole name of the game she didn't and wasn't about to back off.

However, when Nash shoved into her ass this time, he did it with more speed and depth than the last. And Cree followed with a stroke into her pussy right after.

It seemed that each time they retreated and advanced they increased the speed of their pumping hips a little more, until their bodies were slapping against hers.

Violet shook as the pleasurable heated friction of their stroking cocks had the coil deep inside of her priming faster and faster. She'd thought the build-up would be slower since none of them were touching her clit, but that wasn't the case. She was racing headlong toward the biggest orgasm she'd had yet, and although it was a little scary, she didn't fight it.

She tightened her grip around the base of Wilder's cock and bobbed her head faster, and then she cupped his balls in her other hand. Wilder made a weird groaning, growly sound, and when she glanced up at him, her heart skipped a beat. He and his brothers were so damn sexy. Wilder had his head tipped back, his mouth open as he gasped for air, and his muscles were pumped as if he'd been lifting weights. The tendons in his neck stood out starkly under his skin and his eyes were closed.

Elation raced through her heart and soul. She was the reason he was feeling so much pleasure. Violet Evans, who'd never been interested in or had sex until she'd met these wonderful caring men. Determination to make Wilder climax before she did, surged into her with a confidence she'd never thought to feel.

As she slid her mouth back over his cock, she gently rolled his testes and sucked her cheeks in. She savored the taste of his essence on her tongue and the heat emanating from his dick as it pulsed and began to expand.

Violet realized Wilder was about to climax.

But then she was the one hovering on the cusp of ecstasy.

She'd been so intent on Wilder and trying to make him orgasm, she'd only been vaguely aware of Cree caressing his way over her belly and down toward her mound.

She moaned when the tip of Cree's finger brushed over her clit and then groaned as Nash pinched both of her nipples between his fingers and thumbs.

That was all it took.

Violet screamed as she catapulted into rapture.

She shook and shivered as her internal muscles clamped down around the two hard cocks still shuttling in and out of her ass and pussy.

The words Wilder spoke seemed to come from a long way off, but she was glad for the warning. "I'm going to come, sweetness. Pull off."

Violet ignored the warning as she bobbed down as far as she could without choking herself as she gently squeezed his balls.

Wilder roared just before his cock expanded, and then he was spuming cum into the back of her mouth. Violet gulped down his juices relishing the taste of his salty-sweet jism as she swallowed and continued to climax herself.

Wilder eased his spent cock from her mouth and dropped to the bed with a grunt.

Her whole body quaked and quivered, her pussy and ass muscles contracting and releasing around their pistoning dicks.

Nash was grunting and panting behind her, still plucking and rolling her nipples as he continued to fuck her ass. As he withdrew the next time he made a low groaning sound, and as he shoved forward again, he shouted.

He ground his pelvis against her ass and climaxed.

Violet's orgasm was just starting to wane, but just as she opened her eyes to meet Cree's gaze, he took her clit between his finger and thumb and squeezed firmly.

She tried to scream as she tumbled over into another orgasm before the last had completely diminished.

Violet saw stars. This climax was more intense than the last, and she felt as if she'd lost total control of her body. Her inner muscles spasmed with powerful contractions and cream gushed from her pussy. White sheeted in front of her eyes and then she felt as if she was falling.

Lassitude stole into her muscles and she grunted when she fell onto Cree's chest. Cree shouted, his cock pulsing and twitching in her pussy, enhancing the aftershocks still wracking her body. The bright light faded, and for a moment she thought she was going to pass out. But thankfully the darkness forming in front of her eyes dissipated.

She lay over Cree supine with lethargic satiation as she tried to recover her strength and breath. Goose bumps raced over her skin as Cree, Wilder, and Nash caressed over her body, easing her down from such an intense rapturous high.

Violet shivered and her muscles contracted. She gasped with shock. She'd just come so hard the top of her head had almost blown off, and here was her body twitching with interest again.

That was when she realized how very special her three men were and that she'd already fallen deeply in love with them.

While she was happy, she was also scared.

Violet just hoped that nothing happened to ruin this budding relationship because if it did, she wasn't sure she'd ever be whole again.

Chapter Fourteen

"You look happy," Enya said the moment Violet entered the diner kitchen.

"I am." She smiled back.

"Those men are good for you." Enya regarded her speculatively. "There's a twinkle in your eye that wasn't there before."

Violet nodded and hoped her cheeks weren't as red as they felt as she remembered the passion her and her men had shared the night before. Wilder, Cree, and Nash had made love to her together for the second time, and they made her feel so much pleasure she had passed out.

When she'd come to, it was to find three very worried men staring at her. The relief she'd seen in their gazes as she reassured them that she was better than fine had brought tears to her eyes, as had the love she could see in their gorgeous green orbs.

They hadn't said the words yet, but Violet had a feeling it was only a matter of time before they did and she was ready to respond in kind.

Violet glanced at Enya and frowned when she saw the dark smudges beneath her eyes. It was only then she realized that she didn't think she'd ever seen the other woman smile. She mentally shook her head. Enya did smile and laugh when they were all chatting and mucking around, but it seemed forced. Sometimes Enya looked as if she had the weight of the world on her shoulders.

She pushed her introspection away when Cindy called, "Order up," and grabbed the ticket from the slot and read over it.

"Why aren't you in school?" Vi asked as she met Cindy's gaze.

"It's a student free day." Cindy smiled.

"Oh. Okay then. You should have taken the opportunity to catch up on some homework."

Cindy huffed out a breath, and when her face started to turn pink, she glanced away. "I've finished it all."

"Why does that embarrass you?" Vi frowned.

"Some of the other kids like to tease me about being a good student."

"Don't let them get to you, honey," she said as she flipped the steak on the grill. "They'll be the ones who have less choices in college if they even manage to get their high school diplomas. People like that usually only tease and bully because they're jealous."

"Uh, I hadn't thought of it like that." Cindy met her gaze and smiled. "Thanks, Vi, you're the best."

"No, I'm not, but thanks for saying it anyway."

As she cooked she thought about Wilder, Cree, and Nash. The last four days had been the best of Violet's life. She spent all of her free time with her men.

They'd started working as deputies, and while she worried about some of the hazards they were certain to face, she would never ask them to do something else. The more time she spent with them, the more she got to know them. They fit into Slick Rock like peas in a pod, because most of the men living in this town were very protective, so it wasn't a surprise that Wilder, Cree, and Nash wanted to move here or join law enforcement. They were alpha type men, but also honest and noble, and they hated to see an injustice done. Being deputy sheriffs was the perfect job for them, and she was confident they could take care of themselves while dealing with criminals since they were retired Marines.

By the time Violet had finished her shift at the diner, she was exhausted. She'd spent the last four nights at her men's house making love to them for hours on end. And while she gloried in their loving as much as they had, she wasn't sure she could keep up the pace. She was tender in a lot of intimate places, and the muscles in her legs and hips were a little stiff and sore. Add in the long hours she'd been standing while cooking for the diner's customers, and she was weary to the bone.

She'd thought about calling her guys and telling them she would walk home after work so she could stretch some of those muscles out, but sighed with resignation. There was no way the Sheffield brothers would let her walk the dark streets of Slick Rock alone, and to be honest she didn't think she had the energy.

Violet locked up and met Cree at the back door to the truck. He kissed her lightly on the lips and lifted her into the cab before climbing in after her.

"How was your day, honey?" Cree asked.

"Good. Long." She sighed as she closed her eyes. "How was your day? Did you catch any bad guys?"

Nash turned to gaze at her over his shoulder from the front passenger seat and smiled at her. "No, it was a pretty uneventful day. There was an accident out of the freeway, but thankfully no one was hurt. We were needed to direct traffic around the scene so the looky-loos didn't hold everyone up."

"Do you all usually work together?" Vi asked as she gazed at Wilder. Although he'd glanced at her in the rearview mirror a few times, he hadn't spoken a word. From the way his jaw was clenched tight, something was bothering him.

"No," Nash answered. "We're usually on our own, but sometimes more of us are needed to deal with situations."

"Luke was talking about pairing us up," Cree said. "This town is growing so fast and there's more crime than there used to be. He and Damon want us all to work in twos from next week on."

"That makes sense. At least y'all will have backup on hand all the time, rather than having to wait for it in a dangerous situation."

Nash nodded. "We think so, too, baby. I can tell you're exhausted. Why don't you close your eyes?"

Violet met Wilder's gaze in the mirror again and frowned when he quickly glanced away. Maybe when they got home in a few minutes, he'd tell them all what was wrong. She leaned her head against the back of the seat and yawned.

Although she hadn't been dozing while Wilder drove, Vi hadn't been able to keep her heavy eyelids open either. With a tired sigh, she opened her eyes and reached for the door handle.

"Stay where you are, honey," Cree said. "I'll come around and help you out."

"Okay," Vi replied, too tired to move just yet.

Cree opened the door and scooped her up into his arms. Violet glanced over at her cottage, thinking about the laundry and cleaning she needed to do, but she didn't protest as Cree carried her into their house.

"Why don't I just take you straight to bed, honey? You can barely keep your eyes open."

While she was aware of Nash and Wilder coming inside and closing the door, she kept her gaze on Cree's as she tried to decide what to do. As much as she wanted to sleep between them, she'd been neglecting her own place, and she knew if she stayed with them she would only end up wanting to make love with them.

With a resigned sigh, she shook her head and wiggled out of Cree's arms. He frowned at her as he set her feet on the floor and then dropped his arms to his sides. She flopped onto the sofa, just after Cree sat. Cree draped an arm around her shoulders and pulled her against his side. "I don't think that's a good idea." Violet covered her mouth as she yawned.

"Why the hell not?" Wilder snarled his question as he stormed toward her.

Violet gasped and blinked at him with shock. Wilder hadn't said a word as he drove them all home and now he was snarling at her. *What the fuck?*

She crossed her arms beneath her breasts and glared at him before glancing toward Cree and Nash. They were both frowning at Wilder, too.

* * * *

Cree had no idea what had ticked Wilder off, but he had a feeling it had something to do with the phone call he had received from Luke as they'd waited for Violet. He hadn't even said hi to their woman when she'd gotten into the car, and from the way he'd been grinding his teeth and gripping the steering wheel until his knuckles had turned white, Wilder was pissed.

He scowled at his brother when Violet tensed and crossed her arms over her chest, but Wilder had his gaze locked with their woman's and wasn't taking any notice of him. However, he didn't think that there was any way Wilder could miss Cree's glare when he was sitting right next to Violet.

"You all have work tomorrow just as I do. I need to get up early to go shopping for the diner, and then I have to work through lunch and dinner. I haven't spent a single night in my own house and have chores that need doing as well."

"What's that got to do with anything?" Wilder snapped.

Cree couldn't let Wilder continue talking to Violet that way. He lifted his arm from around her shoulder and shoved to his feet, before walking closer to his brother. "What the fuck crawled up your ass?"

Nash must have been of the same mind because he stood, too. "What the fuck is your problem?"

"I can't deal with this shit," Wilder shouted just before he turned away and walked toward his bedroom, slamming the door behind him.

Cree scrubbed a hand over his face and turned toward Violet. His heart flipped in his chest when he saw pain and tears in her eyes. She had her purse over her arm and was racing toward the front door.

"Violet, wait. Please don't leave, honey."

She swallowed audibly and shook her head. She gazed down the hallway before looking at Nash and then him, again. She opened her mouth as if she was about to say something and then shook her head again before she raced out the front door.

Cree followed her out and stood on the porch as she hurried toward her own house. He wanted to go after her and calm her down, but he had no idea what to say. He didn't know what Wilder's problem was, but he was sure as fuck about to find out.

Cree hoped that Wilder hadn't just ruined their chances of a relationship with Violet. If his brother had screwed things up for all of them, he wasn't sure he'd ever be able to forgive him.

* * * *

Wilder was so out of control he wanted to punch something. He also felt guilty as hell for reacting that way in front of Violet. He'd seen the hurt in her eyes just before he'd turned away, but his gut was in knots and he didn't know what to do.

Normally he was the calmest out of his brothers, but after what Luke had told him over the phone, he was so full of rage he hadn't been able to contain it. He hadn't had the chance to explain to his brothers what was going on because he'd only just ended the call with Luke when Vi had exited the diner.

His bedroom door burst open so hard the door handle crashed into the wall behind it, denting the plaster. Cree and Nash stormed into the room and glared at him.

"What the fuck, Wilder?" Nash shouted.

"Do you have any idea what you've just done," Cree roared. "Violet left in tears, and from the way she was hurting I don't think she'll ever want to come back."

"I wouldn't blame her if she didn't," Nash snarled. "If you fucked everything up for us with her, I'll never fucking forgive you."

Wilder sank down and sat on the edge of his bed. He scrubbed a hand over his face and sighed. His heart was hurting so much he ended up rubbing his chest. "I'm sorry."

"You should be fucking sorry," Cree yelled. "But you should be apologizing to Violet, not us."

"I know." Wilder nodded.

"Care to explain what that was all about?" Nash asked in a calmer voice.

"IA sent their report to Luke."

"And?" Cree asked.

"The sheriff of Bemidji and his deputy were actually living at the cult."

"What?" Nash's voice was hoarse with shock. "Are you fucking kidding me?"

Wilder shook his head. "I wish I was."

"How did they get caught?" Cree walked over and sat on the bed.

"IA had an undercover detective trailing the assholes."

"Fuck!"

"Yeah." Wilder rubbed the back of his neck. "Those fuckers were claiming welfare using the names of deceased people, and they were working as lawmen. I'm sure we don't know the half of it, but there were six women being held against their will. They were being raped nearly every day. They've been held hostage for fifteen to twenty years."

"Geezus."

"What about the girls Violet grew up with? Were they there?"

Wilder nodded. "Once the detective had enough to raid the place and arrest everyone, the house and land was searched thoroughly. They brought in sniffer dogs, too. They found a woman's bones buried near the border of the land."

"Fuck." Cree shook his head.

Wilder shoved to his feet and began to pace. "Those motherfuckers were supposed to serve and protect. They ignored a young girl's call for help because they were in it up to their necks. How the fuck are we going to tell Violet?"

"We can't keep this from her, Wilder," Nash said. "She'll probably have to give evidence when those bastards are brought to trial."

"I know," Wilder replied loudly before taking a deep breath as he tried to calm down. "This is going to kill her."

"It'll be hard, but we'll be by her side. We have to tell her before she sees it on the news," Cree explained.

"Shit. I didn't even think of the media." Wilder hurried toward the door.

"Stop." Nash surged to his feet and moved to block his brother. "You need to give her time to calm down. Tomorrow will be soon enough for you to apologize. Hopefully, when she accepts your apology, we can explain what's going on."

Wilder nodded even though he didn't want to put off his apology to Violet. But she'd been exhausted, so he gave in and agreed with his brother.

Cree and Nash told him good night and headed toward their own rooms.

Wilder got ready for bed but had a feeling he wouldn't be getting much sleep. His mind was racing in circles, and he was used to cuddling up with Violet. Because he'd let his anger rule his emotions, he was going to spend a long lonely night on his own.

Hopefully, when he apologized tomorrow night after explaining his outburst, she would have it in her heart to forgive him.

Wilder rubbed at the knot of anxiety tightening his chest. The hair on his nape had been itching since Luke's call. Even though he knew why he was feeling antsy, he just couldn't seem to settle down.

He tried pushing his internal alarm aside so he could sleep, and first thing tomorrow he would go and see Violet.

He just hoped that she didn't slam her door in his face like he deserved.

Chapter Fifteen

"Damn it," Violet sobbed as she stared at herself in the mirror.

She hadn't slept a wink last night. Her heart felt as if it had been ripped out her chest only to leave a gaping hole behind. She was hurting and she'd cried so much she'd ended up vomiting.

She'd just taken a shower, brushed her hair and teeth, and even though she'd applied a light amount of makeup to her face, it couldn't hide her bloodshot eyes or how swollen they were. The only consolation was that she'd got all her chores done while blubbering her eyes out.

Now she needed to go to the supermarket and pick up the things Delta had ordered a few days ago, but that hadn't been delivered since the ingredients had been out of stock. Maybe after that she would just hang around the diner until it was time for her shift to start. If she stayed home, she was only going to end up having another pity party over Wilder breaking up with her.

She had no idea what she'd done wrong to make him say what he had, but she wasn't about to beg him and his brothers to take her back.

Violet had seen how men treated women, and while she now bemoaned her decision to try a relationship with the Sheffield men and what the consequences were, if she could do it all over, she didn't think she'd change anything.

Although she was hurting, she was proud of herself for taking that risky step even though everything had gone to shit.

Hopefully, in time she'd be able to put this behind her and think of them with fond memories, but right now, she didn't want to think of them at all. It just hurt too damn much.

Violet glanced at her watch and then hurried from the bathroom. She needed to get out of here and fast because she had a feeling Wilder, Cree, and Nash would be knocking on her door any minute. If that happened, she wasn't sure what she would do.

After snagging her purse from the counter, she hurried toward the door and locked up behind her. She couldn't seem to stop herself from glancing over at their house. Thank goodness all was quiet because she had to blink the tears from her eyes again.

Shoring up her defenses with a deep breath, she powerwalked toward the town center and hoped that there wouldn't be too many people around at this time of the morning. She wasn't in the right frame of mind to be friendly, but she was determined to have her emotions under control when she got to the diner.

Forty-five minutes later she entered the diner kitchen and began to put the shopping away and tried to ignore the looks Delta and Enya were giving her. When she was done, she poured herself a cup of coffee and sat on the stool beside the industrial-sized fridge.

"What's wrong?" Enya and Delta asked at the same time.

"Nothing. Just had trouble sleeping."

"You look as if you haven't slept at all." Enya frowned.

She glanced over to find Delta frowning as she scrutinized her face.

"What did they do?" Delta asked.

And just like that Violet fell apart again. Enya and Delta rushed over and hugged her between them as she cried. Great tearing sobs wracked her body and she began to feel sick again. Violet called on all her self-control and with steely determination forced the tears away. She wiped the back of her hands over her cheeks and gratefully took the paper towel Enya handed over and blew her nose.

"Tell us what happened," Enya demanded as she stepped back, her hands resting on her hips.

Once Violet finished telling her friends and business partners what the deal was, they both looked mad as hell. Warmth at having such good friends surged into her heart, easing some of the pain and emptiness, but she knew that only Wilder, Cree, and Nash would ever be able to fill that hole. She was just going to have to get used to walking around incomplete.

"If they have the audacity to come in here, they're in for a big surprise," Delta signed quickly. "I'm going to spread the word that they aren't go be served."

Violet almost smiled at Delta's anger. She was showing her that no matter what happened, she had a friend for life, but she couldn't let her do something like that for her. If word spread that they were ignoring customers, the good reputation they were building would be ruined.

"Thank you, but I don't want you to do that," Vi said.

"Why the hell not?" Enya snarled. "It would be what they deserved."

"This is a small town and rumors spread. Our business could suffer."

"Shit! I hate it when you're right." Enya huffed and crossed her arms over her chest. "This is why I'll never, ever get involved with a man. They only ever cause pain."

Violet frowned when a flash of pain crossed Enya's gaze and was about to ask if she was all right, but Kiara and Katie entered ready for their shift. She decided to finish her coffee in the office and make sure all the books were up to date so that Delta didn't have to.

Violet spent six hours going through emails, filling in expenses and profits, and making lists for the diner's next delivery. When she noticed it was five minutes to one and her shift was about to start, she stood up and groaned as she stretched.

She'd totally zoned out while she was working, and though she'd been aware of first Enya bringing her more coffee and then Delta entering with more of the same and a sandwich, she'd barely lifted her head.

She had no idea how she was going to get through the afternoon and night, but since she didn't have a choice, she forced herself to walk toward the kitchen.

When she heard the rumble of a familiar voice, she spun on her heels and raced back to the office. Her heart was beating a hundred miles an hour and aching all over again, and while she wanted to see Wilder's handsome face again, she wasn't ready to face him yet. She felt like a coward as she stood just inside the doorway to the office and wished she was a little closer so she could hear what he was saying, but again, she wasn't ready.

He'd hurt her and she wasn't sure she could ever forgive him. How was she supposed to stay in Slick Rock and see him, Cree, and Nash every day and not fall apart? If she hadn't signed a rental lease on her small cottage house or a contract as part owner of the diner, she wouldn't hesitate to pack up the few things she had and move.

Maybe in time she'd be able to think about them without the piercing pain and knee-buckling grief, but she had a feeling it was going to take a long, long time.

Violet startled when Enya entered the office, with Delta on her heels.

"Who's cooking?" she asked.

"The meals can wait a few minutes," Enya answered.

"Violet, I think you need to hear them out," Delta signed.

"Why would you say that? Wilder doesn't want to have anything to do with me. I'm not about to hang around like a bad smell or come between triplets."

Delta held her hand up and then took a deep breath before she began signing again. "I think all this is just a big misunderstanding."

"I agree," Enya said.

Vi frowned at them. Enya had just contradicted her earlier statement of how she wanted nothing to do with the opposite sex.

"Wilder looks as if he's grieving, Vi," Enya said. "Cree and Nash look just as bad."

"That doesn't change what he said."

"It doesn't," Delta replied. "I've spent a little time with them since they're friends and cousins with Major, Rocco, and Ace. They're not the type of men to lead a woman on. Most of the guys in this town are up front and honest. Maybe something bad happened at work, but there is no way Wilder and his brothers would walk away from you after they've told you they wanted a relationship with you."

"You don't know that." Violet frowned.

"Actually, I, we do." Delta pointed toward Enya. "You need to hear them out, Vi."

"What have you got to lose?" Enya asked. "You're already in love with them. Isn't it worth trying to work out your problems?"

"How do you know I love them?"

Delta and Enya glanced at each other and smiled before turning to look at her again.

"You've been so damn happy over the last week it's almost sickening." Enya winked to let her know she was yanking her chain, mostly. "When you talk about them, I can hear the love in your voice each time you say their names. And then there's the dreamy look on your face, and the way you smile every time you think about them."

"Give them a chance, Vi. You've got nothing to lose and everything to gain. They love you, girlfriend. They wouldn't be grieving for you if they didn't, nor would they be trying to set things right." Delta squeezed her hand before turning and leaving the room.

"I'm the last person that would be trying to set you up to be hurt by a man, or in this town's case, men. They really do love you, Violet. Let them explain, apologize, and then get on with your lives. Don't let your pain and anger ruin what could be your one and only chance of a lifetime of happiness."

Violet stared at Enya's back as she hurried back to the kitchen. Enya hardly ever said boo about anything unless it was cooking or the diner. And while she was worried, she also knew that the other women were right. She needed to give Wilder a chance to explain and then she would make a decision on whether she was going to forgive him or not.

* * * *

Wilder was glad for once that he didn't have to ride in the patrol car with his brothers. The tension in the house between the three of them had been so thick, he could have cut it with a knife. They were all worried about Violet. He'd gone over to her house that morning just after seven to apologize, but she hadn't answered his knock on the door. He'd been so concerned about her, he'd peered in the windows only to find she wasn't home. He'd called her cell phone and left texts, but she hadn't responded. It had been hard for him to sit on his hands and not go looking for her, but Cree and Nash had talked him into giving her some time alone to cool off after his hurtful words.

However, he'd decided to try and catch her at the diner before he started his shift, and while he was relieved to find out she was there and safe, Delta and Enya had told him to leave, that Violet didn't want to see him. Her rejection had hurt worse than anything he'd ever felt before—even taking a bullet in the arm while serving in the Marines—but he wasn't giving up. He was going to get her back even if he had to go down on his knees and beg while kissing her feet.

He'd been patrolling the county for over four hours and was scheduled for his meal break soon, so he made a U-turn and headed back to town. Hopefully, Violet would give him a few minutes of her time so he could explain his uncharacteristic behavior the night before. As he drove toward town he tried to figure what he was going to say and wondered if he should tell her everything or just say he'd received some bad news. He didn't want her getting more upset than she already was when she still had to deal with the dinner rush hour. He shook his head.

If he and his brothers were going to build a solid relationship with Violet, there couldn't be any secrets no matter how upsetting the news was. Wilder was going to have to come clean about everything. Including the fact that one of the male cult members had managed to dodge being arrested since he'd been missing.

Just thinking about that sick fuck running around the streets of America was enough to turn his stomach. Wilder, his brothers, the sheriffs, and the other deputies were all on the lookout for Virgil Kennedy as were the other men in town. Everyone was on alert and an MMS message had been sent out with the asshole's license photo on it, but the picture had been taken almost ten years ago. Wilder was worried that the fucker could have changed his appearance and was already in town. The hair on the back of his neck had been on end since last night, and no matter how hard he tried to push the disconcerting feeling aside, it wouldn't budge.

Hopefully, after he'd apologized he and his brothers would be back in Violet's good graces, and she would be back in their arms where they could keep her safe.

Half an hour later Wilder pulled into a parking space just up from the diner and got out. When his gut tightened with anxiety he glanced around but he didn't see anyone watching him so he pushed the feeling aside and strode toward his woman. He nodded to a few men he knew and waved to Major, Ace, Rocco, and Delta, but he didn't detour to do the niceties. He was a man on a mission. The most important mission of his life and he wasn't leaving until he had the results he wanted. Violet back in his arms.

His gaze zeroed in on her as soon as he entered the diner kitchen, and after making sure they were alone, he slowly moved toward her. She must have seen him from the corner of her eye or she'd felt his eyes on her, because she spun on her heels, stirring spoon in hand.

As soon as she met his gaze her expression blanked and her face paled even more, if that was all possible, and his heart slammed against his sternum.

He'd planned what he was going to say while he was driving, but that all went out the window when he noticed her beautiful mauve eyes were bloodshot and the dark smudges beneath them she'd tried to conceal with makeup.

Wilder didn't think about what he was doing, but went on pure instinct and took to his knees. "I'm so sorry for hurting you, sweetness. I'm sorry I took my anger out on you and I'm sorry for what I said. My ire had nothing to do with you, but I took it out on you anyway. Can you ever forgive me?"

Violet set the spoon into the spoon rest and then crossed her arms beneath her breasts as she gazed down into his eyes. A flash of pain crossed her face but was quickly gone again. "Why? Why did you do and say that?"

Wilder got back to his feet, clasped her hand in his, and started explaining. When he'd told her about Luke's late-night phone call after his boss had received an email from the IA undercover cop, and what had transpired in Werner, Minnesota, she swayed on her feet.

He didn't hesitate to pull her into his arm and hold her as she gasped for breath and then started crying. He didn't say anything to placate her, just simply held her. After a few moments she sniffed, scrubbed at her face, and drew out of his arms. She turned to the stove, turned the heat down, and then said, "I need a couple of minutes to clean up."

Wilder rubbed at the back of his neck as he watched her hurry out and hoped that when she came back into the kitchen, she'd be ready to forgive him. The whole time she was gone, he was on tenterhooks and felt as if he couldn't breathe.

When she returned, she walked right up to him and poked him in the chest. "I understand you were angry, upset, but there was no need for you to take it out on me." She paused to clear her throat, and when she drew in a deep breath, he felt like a real asshole when her lower lip trembled. "When you said, 'I can't deal with this shit,' I thought you were referring to me. I thought you wanted to break up with me."

"Fuck! Never, sweetness. I never thought that. How could I when I love you so damn much?"

"You love me?" Violet asked with wonder.

"Yes. More than I could ever tell you, Vi. You're my heart and soul, sweetness."

Wilder wanted to scoop her up into his arms, carry her out of the diner, and spirit her away to his home where he could spend the rest of the night making love to her and telling her with his body how much she meant to him, but that wasn't possible since they both still had to work.

Violet reached up and cupped his cheek in her small, soft hand. "I love you, too, Wilder."

He groaned as he wrapped an arm around her waist while he gripped her ass with his other hand and lifted her off her feet, and then he kissed her passionately.

If Jaylynn hadn't entered the kitchen and cleared her throat, Wilder wasn't sure he'd have been able to stop.

Violet pulled from his arms, blushing up a storm, and he was glad to see the happiness back in those beautiful lilac eyes.

"Cindy's half an hour late and I'm worried. She's never late," Jaylynn said.

"Have you tried calling her cell phone?" Violet frowned.

"Yes, and her house phone, but no one answered."

Violet turned her gaze to his. He could see the concern in her eyes.

"Do you have her address on file, sweetness? Wilder asked.

"Yes, in the office." Violet rushed toward the door and he followed.

She rifled through the filing cabinet. When she found what she was looking for, she handed him Cindy's personal details.

"I'll call as soon as I find out what's going on." Wilder pressed a quick kiss to her lips and strode out toward his patrol car. He hoped that Cindy was okay, but from the way his gut was roiling, he wasn't sure he was going to have good news to give to Violet.

Chapter Sixteen

It had been half an hour since Wilder had left, and while she was happy that he'd apologized and they were okay again, Violet was very worried about Cindy.

When her phone vibrated in her pocket, she sighed with relief, dropped what she was doing, and tugged her cell out. After activating the screen with a swipe of her finger, she touched the message app icon and started reading.

Fear skittered up her spine when she read the text. It was from Cindy's phone, but she knew that the teenager hadn't sent her the message.

I have the girl. If you want to save her, come to the abandoned warehouse behind the motel. Don't tell anyone where you're going or what you're doing if you want the slut to live.

Violet had no compunction about leaving the diner full of people waiting for their meals. While no names were mentioned, she knew deep in her gut that "the girl" was Cindy. Nothing mattered but getting her back. She had no idea who'd sent the message, and while she wanted to forward it to Wilder, Cree, and Nash, she didn't want to put Cindy's life in jeopardy.

No, she had to do this alone. There was no way she was going to do something that would get Cindy hurt. Or worse, killed.

"Jaylynn, I know this is asking a lot, but I need to rush to the store. Can you cover things while I'm gone?"

Violet didn't need to be a mind reader to know the other woman was taken aback. Thankfully Katie was still serving and taking orders out front, so hopefully no one waiting for meals would be the wiser. Everything that was listed on the special boards was simmering or being kept warm in the ovens. The only thing Jaylynn would need to cook was steak if it was ordered and hamburgers.

"Why don't tell me what you need and I'll go to the store?" Jaylynn suggested.

Violet mentally cursed. Why did Jaylynn have to be smart and come up with a logical suggestion? Her mind was blank, and while she hoped she wasn't showing her anxiety, she was frantic and scared inside.

"I can't explain to you why, but I need to leave. Now!"

Jaylynn nodded and though Violet could tell she wasn't happy about the situation, she was relieved she wasn't kicking up a fuss. She quickly showed her where everything was and then pulled her into a hug.

"Thank you. I'll make this up to you. I promise." Violet released Jaylynn and ran toward her office. There was no way she was wasting precious time. She tugged the desk drawer open and was about to grab her purse, but quickly slammed it shut again. It had been an automatic response to going somewhere, but she didn't have a need to take it with her.

Violet ran out of the office toward the back door and exited. As she ran to the east side of Slick Rock, she prayed whoever had Cindy would release her as soon as she showed up. Her lungs were burning, but it wasn't just because she was running. It was because she was scared shitless.

It took her ten minutes to get where she needed to be, but it felt much longer. She stopped and stared at the dark, abandoned warehouse while she tried to regain her breath and gnawed on her lower lip as she tried to decide what to do. Her cell was in her pocket, but she had a feeling she would be searched as soon as she stepped inside. Maybe now was the time she should forward that text to Wilder. If she did, he, Cree, and Nash might be able to pinpoint her using her phone's GPS.

After tugging the phone from her pocket, she activated the screen and brought up the nefarious message she'd received about Cindy and then she forwarded it to Wilder. She fumbled and nearly dropped it when she was trying to put her phone on silent, but caught it just in time.

Violet thought about putting the cell down her jeans or tucking it into her bra, but she was so scared it would be found she decided to hide it behind the stack of bricks just beside the side door. Hopefully, her guys wouldn't take too long to find her.

Tears burned her eyes, her heart slammed painfully against her ribs, and she was having trouble breathing, but she shoved her terror down after taking a few deep breaths then holding them, before releasing them slowly. She had to do this for Cindy's sake.

She took a step toward the ajar tin door and was just about to reach out to open it further, when a large hand wrapped around her wrist. Violet screamed as she dropped her phone to the side, trying to cover up what she was doing and prayed that she hadn't done permanent damage as it hit the ground. If her cell was smashed, she was screwed.

She moaned with pain as the side of her head hit the edge of the door as she saw stars, and then she was being dragged into the building. Violet tried to breathe and blink away the wooziness in her head as she stumbled behind whoever was dragging her. Even though she dug her heels in and tried to slow the asshole down, it didn't seem to affect him.

Finally, her vision cleared and she glanced around the interior. It was big and dark, and although there were no lights on, there were skylights which let in enough moonlight for her to see some.

Her breath sobbed out of her mouth when she saw Cindy tied to a chair with silver tape across her mouth. The right side of her face was bruised and swollen and her head was hanging down.

"Cindy," Violet called as she tried to escape the guys clutches yet again, but he just laughed and tightened his hold on her wrist until she felt the bones move. She gasped with pain and hoped he didn't end up breaking her wrist.

Cindy lifted her head and gazed at her through her left eye. The right was too swollen to open. When the young girl started crying and shaking her head, Violet's fear turned to rage. She tried to get her balance so she could fight and get away from the asshole, but she almost ended up tripping and falling to her knees when he yanked on her arm.

And then he stopped—right under one of the plastic skylights in the metal roof—and he turned to face her.

The anger waned and terror took its place. Violet began to quake with fear as she stared into the familiar face she'd hoped never to see again.

* * * *

Wilder cursed after looking into all the windows of the dark house. He'd known there was no one home as soon as he pulled up outside of Cindy's house, but he'd had to check just to make sure. When he'd tried the handle to the back door, he'd cursed some more under his breath just in case there was someone hiding inside. The door was unlocked. He'd entered the house and searched room by room, but didn't find anything.

Wilder pulled his cell phone from his pocket and glanced at the paper that had Cindy's personal information on it. When he saw the emergency name and contact, he started dialing. Thankfully, Wendy, Cindy's mother, answered on the first ring.

"Hello, Mrs. Dodge, this is Deputy Wilder Sheffield. I'm at your house looking for Cindy since she didn't show up for her shift at the diner."

"What? Oh, my god."

"Do you have any idea where your daughter might be?"

"No," Mrs. Dodge sobbed. "Cindy's a good girl. She never shirks her responsibilities. Something had to have happened."

"Can you give me the names of the people she hangs out with?" Wilder had trouble understanding the distraught woman when she answered.

"Cindy isn't like normal teenagers. She's a good girl. She goes to school and always comes straight home. If she's not working or studying, she's in her room reading and babysitting her deaf sister. She's never invited anyone home and only ever talks about the people she works with."

"Where are you, Mrs. Dodge?" Wilder asked.

"I'm at work. I fill the shelves at the supermarket after it closes."

"Please, try and stay calm. I'm going to send one of the deputies to pick you up and take you back to the station. They'll ask you some questions which may help us to locate your daughter."

"Please, find my baby," Mrs. Dodge wailed.

"I'll do my best, ma'am." Wilder hurried out the back door, making sure to lock it behind him, and once he was in his car, he informed dispatch what was going on. Just as he was about to start the ignition, his cell buzzed with an incoming text. He smiled when he saw Violet's name, but when he read the message he roared with fury.

Wilder hit the call button and waited impatiently for Violet to answer. It seemed to take forever for the phone to ring out before her voice mail message cut in. He didn't bother trying to call again, but called the phone at the diner instead. Jaylynn answered sounding breathless and flustered.

"Jaylynn, it's Wilder. Can I talk to Violet?"

"She's not here."

When a loud roaring set up in his ears and fear skittered up his spine, he didn't have to ask Jaylynn to repeat what she'd said after those first terrifying three words. Nor did he bother ending the call politely, he just hung up on her.

He once more informed dispatch of the situation and then conferenced called his brothers. Wilder's gut was churning and the hair on his nape was standing on end. His hand shook as he combed his fingers through his hair and explained to his brothers what was going on.

"Are you fucking kidding me?" Cree roared.

"Fuck!" Nash snarled.

"I'm on my way," his brothers said simultaneously.

Wilder nodded as he pressed his foot down hard on the gas pedal after starting his patrol car. "Don't turn your lights or sirens on. We don't want to alert the bastard we're coming."

"We know what to and what not to do, Wilder," Cree snapped.

Wilder knew Cree wasn't really angry with him. His brothers were scared for their woman just as he was. "Nash, do you have any rappelling equipment in your truck?"

"You should know the answer to that. I always carry that gear with me."

"Good. We'll meet at the entrance end of the street and go in the rest of the way on foot. We don't want to scare this fucker into running or worse." Wilder took a deep breath and tried to calm his tumultuous emotions. He and his brothers were going to be the cold killing Marines they'd been trained to be. If they let their fear and other emotions take over, they could end up making a mistake which could get Cindy and Violet killed.

Cold hard determination filled his heart and soul. He and his brothers were going to save Cindy and Violet, even if they had to take a bullet to do it.

* * * *

Violet's knees were shaking so badly she wasn't sure how she was still standing. Her worst nightmare was standing right in front of her. As she looked into those evil emotionless eyes, she tried to think of what to do. It was hard to get her terror under control so she could process everything logically, but she needed to do it for Cindy. There was no way she was letting this fucker hurt another innocent girl.

But as hard as she tried, nothing came to mind.

And then everything changed. She saw Wilder's, Cree's, and Nash's faces as they gazed at her with so much love in their eyes it made her own burn with tears. Violet had only just found the loves of her life, and she wasn't about to let this bastard destroy everything.

She glanced over at Cindy to see her sobbing quietly, and her psyche filled with resolve. Violet would give up her own life if it meant the young woman came out of this alive. She envisaged her men again, hoping that they felt her love and sorrow as she thought of them, and then she shoved her fear away. A calmness and confidence she'd never felt before settled over her, and she turned her gaze back to his.

Virgil Kennedy was going down if it was the last thing she did.

* * * *

Wilder had arrived at their meeting site way before his brothers, since he'd already been in town, and he took the opportunity to reconnoiter around the empty warehouse. Other than the side door which had been locked from the inside, the only other entry point was the big sliding door at the front. There was no way he and his brothers could get in there without alerting the kidnapper. The only way he could see inside was through the roof. Thank fuck there was a fire escape leading to the roof; otherwise, they would have had to cut their way in. Again, the noise would have been a dead giveaway.

He ran back toward the street entrance and was relieved to see his brothers pulling up behind his deputy vehicle. Nash and Cree hurried toward him.

"What have you got?" Nash asked.

Wilder beckoned his brothers to the vacant lot on the corner, grabbed his flashlight, turned it on, and then picked up a stick and drew a map in the dirt.

"There are two exits," Wilder explained. "A side door here which is locked from the inside and a large sliding loading door here. They're both out. There must be a mezzanine level inside because there's a fire escape here."

"How are we going to get in through the roof?" Cree asked. "None of us have a laser cutter, welder, or tin snips."

"There are polycarbonate skylights at intervals along the roof. That's going to be the quickest and easiest way to get in."

"The fucker's still going to hear us coming." Nash scrubbed a hand over his face.

"Yeah, but if we do it right, he's not going to have much time to react." Wilder glanced up the street when he heard a vehicles racing toward them. He wasn't at all surprised to see Luke and Damon as well as some other deputies.

"What's the plan?" Luke asked as he came to stand beside Cree. Damon was right beside him. All the men gathered around.

Wilder and his brothers moved back, allowing everyone to see his dirt drawing, and then went over everything again.

Damon nodded. "We'll cover all the exits. There's no way this bastard is getting away."

"Thanks," Wilder nodded at all the men. "Right now, I wish I was still in the Marines."

"What do you need?" Damon asked as he gave Luke a chagrinned glance. "I have a sniper's rifle and some flashbangs in a lock box."

Wilder waited for Luke to curse up a storm, but what came out of the sheriff's mouth surprised even him. "Get them. You go with

Wilder, Cree, and Nash. As soon as they're through the skylights get that fucker in your aim."

"Thank you." Wilder was overwhelmed by their colleague's support and willingness to do anything to save Violet and Cindy even though they'd been a part of the department for less than a week.

"Let's do this," Nash said after grabbing the rappelling gear from his car.

Wilder took point as they jogged down the street. He was in soldier mode, and he kept gazing every which way to make sure there was no one else about. He led Cree, Nash, and Damon to the ladder fire escape and climbed quickly, taking care not to make any noise. Once he was on the roof he waited for Cree, Nash, and Damon, pointing to where he wanted them to go in. He was dropping in first, then Cree and Nash if needed, and he was grateful that Damon would be able to cover them with sniper fire if necessary.

After setting up the rappelling rope and taking one of the flashbang grenades Damon handed him, Wilder drew a deep breath and cleared his mind.

It was time to save his woman and Cindy.

* * * *

Time seemed to slow and race at the same time. Violet glanced at the cruel hand around her wrist, and when she saw where his thumb and finger met, she twisted her arm until they were facing down and then shoved her arm down hard. Elation surged through her when she broke his hold, and she stepped into him instead of fleeing and lifted her knee.

She missed. She had no idea how he'd known what she was going to do, but he'd shifted slightly to the side so that she'd connected with his thigh and not his groin. Violet was so shocked she didn't see the fist coming toward her face until it was too late.

Pain shot into her jaw, neck, and head, and while she tried to remain conscious, the beckoning darkness nearly won. Just as she was getting her awareness back she was shoved to the floor. She would have cried out in pain if she had been able to, but she'd landed on her back and all the air was shoved from her lungs.

Violet was about to roll over and scramble up on all fours, but she didn't get the chance, Virgil was on top of her before she could move. She hit out at him, hoping to hurt him and get him off of her, but he grabbed her wrists and slammed them to the cold concrete beside her head. She bucked and wriggled, kicking out blindly, but he was too strong. He'd given her all of his body weight, and since he was at least four or so inches taller than her and outweighed her by approximately a hundred pounds, she didn't have a hope in hell.

She tried getting her hands away when he grasped both her wrists in one hand, but he didn't seem to notice her puny efforts. When cold enveloped first one wrist and then the other and she heard a click as handcuffs snapped into place, she screamed.

His evil laughter had her swallowing down her revulsion as she stared up at him. He pressed down cruelly on her arms as he pushed up and then laughed even louder as he dropped down hard onto her stomach. Bile rushed up her throat and she turned her head to the side, not wanting to choke on her own vomit if she was sick.

She whimpered when he grabbed the lapel of her blouse and tugged hard. Buttons flew off her shirt and the material parted, exposing her bra-covered breasts. Tears welled, and while she tried to blink them back, they spilled over, trickling over her temples and into her hair.

She could hear Cindy's muffled sobs and yells, but since her mouth was covered she couldn't work out what she was trying to say. Violet cringed when Virgil licked his lips while staring at her breasts.

"You didn't think I'd let you get away with escaping, did you? You were supposed to be mine, slut. I'm going to have what I should have ten years ago."

Virgil reached toward his hip, and when she saw what he was holding, she began to shake. The metal blade glinted under the shine of the weak moonlight. When the knife came toward her, she closed her eyes and waited for the pain. She screamed when the cold metal slipped under her bra between her breasts and held her breath and tensed. A hard tug was all she felt, and when she looked down, her breasts were totally bare. He'd cut through her bra.

Violet closed her eyes and turned her head away when he grabbed first one breast and then the other. This time she bit her tongue to keep her pain-filled cries contained. She wasn't about to give him the satisfaction of knowing he was hurting her. It didn't matter that she would be left with bruises. It didn't matter what he did to her as long as she survived.

She would take anything he did to her and she would fight to live so she could see Wilder's, Cree's, and Nash's handsome faces once more.

Virgil must have gotten distracted when he shifted down to sit on her thighs, because his grip on her wrists loosened. Violet kept her head turned away, but peeked at him from the corner of her eye as she lifted her lids slightly. Her stomach roiled again when she saw him licking his lips as he stared at her mound. He was gazing between her legs so avidly he seemed to be in a trance. The knife clattered to the floor as he reached toward the button on her slacks, and when she felt him tugging them open, she made her move.

Violet didn't stop to think; she just reacted. She brought her knees up, pressed her feet to the floor, and then shoved off of the concrete. Her knees slammed into his back and he started to fall forward, but he caught his weight on the hand he'd been using to get her trousers open.

He roared with anger as he shifted his weight and then slammed his elbow into the side of her head. Agony ripped through her skull, and this time there was no way to fight the enveloping darkness. Just before she sank into unconsciousness, she felt his hands tearing at the rest of her clothes.

* * * *

Cree wanted to be the one to go in first, but didn't object to Wilder taking point. His brother was faster than he was going down a rope, and there was no way he was arguing when Violet was in danger.

He and Nash had gazed at the plastic skylight while Wilder was setting up and anchoring his rope. They'd both decided the best way in was to pry the plastic up from under the metal sheets. If they'd cut through it, whoever was holding Cindy and Violet would have definitely been alerted to their presence.

It was slow going because they were being careful to keep the noise to a minimum, but finally he and Nash lifted the clear panel aside and set it on the roof. Cree donned his gloves to protect his hands from friction burn, and after checking his service weapon, he met Wilder's gaze.

"Ready?" Wilder mouthed the word just in case his voice carried.

Cree nodded as did Nash, and Damon gave him the thumbs-up as he got into position. The hole they'd created was bigger than he'd first thought it would be, but still not big enough for the three of them to descend at the same time.

Wilder must have thought the same thing. He pointed at Cree and nodded toward the rope. "Together," he said in a low monotone that wouldn't carry as he handed the flashbang grenade to Nash.

Cree pointed to his eyes and closed them before meeting Wilder's gaze again. His brother nodded, and then they moved to the edge of the hole. Nash was on his belly on the opposite side to Damon. The sheriff had one eye to the rifle scope as he waited for the countdown. Cree pointed at his eyes again when he turned to face Damon and got a thumbs-up in acknowledgment.

They were good to go.

* * * *

Nash clenched his fist around the grenade and waited for Wilder's go signal. When he heard Violet screaming, and then total silence, fear as he'd never known it coursed through his blood and into his heart. He trembled so hard, he almost dropped the grenade. After leaning over the side to find where Violet and Cindy were being held, he ducked back as he planned where he'd drop the percussion grenade, and as he took a deep steadying breath, he pushed his emotions aside. Nash glanced toward Wilder.

He got his terror under control just in time. Wilder held up three fingers and started dropping them as he counted off. As soon as the last finger curled over, Nash pulled the pin and lobbed the grenade.

He closed his eyes as soon as he hurled it and hoped the others had, too. The deafening explosion made his ears ring even though he wasn't that close to it, but seconds later he opened his eyes again.

Cree and Wilder had already slipped into the hole and were speeding down the ropes. Nash followed seconds later.

His heart nearly burst out of his chest when he saw Violet naked on the floor with the asshole on top of her. He was just about to sprint toward her, but Cree and Wilder got to her first.

Nash searched the room for Cindy, spotting her toward the far end of the building bound to a chair with her arms tied behind her back and her ankles tethered to the legs. Her head was hanging forward, but he could see the silver taped covering her mouth.

He ran toward the young woman, pulling a pocket knife from his belt, and cut her loose. After he had her in his arms, he turned back toward Violet and his brothers.

Cree had the asshole bound with his hands behind his back in handcuffs. Wilder had stripped off his shirt and was in the process of covering Violet's nakedness.

"How is she?" Nash asked once he was close enough for his brothers to hear as he gazed down into Violet's face. He baulked when he saw the swelling and bruises on her face, but it was the dark contusion at her temple that had his earlier fear returning. Tears stung his eyes, and it wasn't until he stared at her chest and saw that she was still breathing that he relaxed slightly. "Did he—" He swallowed around the constriction in his throat and prayed to who would ever listen that they'd gotten to her in time.

Cree swiped at the tears on his face and shook his head. "We got her just as he was about to."

"Thank Christ." Nash turned toward the locked side door when he heard the sirens and guessed that one of the sheriffs or other deputies had called the paramedics.

As he carried Cindy toward the exit behind Wilder, who had Violet in his arms, a litany began to chant through his mind.

Please, let Violet be okay. Please, let Violet be okay.

Please. Please. Please.

Chapter Seventeen

Violet spent a total of five days in the small, new Slick Rock Hospital. She'd ended up with a severe concussion and had spent two of those five days puking her guts up.

While she was aware of Wilder, Cree, and Nash at her bedside, helping to hold her hair when she was sick, giving her water to drink, and just generally taking care of her, she'd been in too much pain and drowsy to ask them any questions. One thing they'd told her had gotten through her pain-wracked brain, though. Cindy was safe.

On the third day she'd been able to ask questions. Her men told her about what had happened to the male members of the cult in Werner and that the Bemidji Sheriff and his deputy had been members, as well.

She couldn't believe she hadn't put two and two together when she'd dreamed about the star man, but she was glad that all those assholes were going to pay for what they'd done.

Virgil Kennedy had been arrested and was facing a slew of felony charges such as rape, kidnapping, holding hostages against their will, as well as fraud and murder.

Although she had regular visitors, her guys hadn't let anyone in to see her other than Cindy. Cindy only spent one night in hospital for observation, and although she said she was fine, Violet knew it was going to take time for the teenager to get over what had happened to her. She'd apologized to Cindy, and though she'd said Violet had nothing to be sorry for, it was hard to not feel guilty. If Virgil hadn't been obsessed with her, none of this would have happened.

Wilder, Cree, and Nash were her rocks as she recovered. They swapped shifts with their fellow deputies so that one of them was with her at all times after she was discharged from the hospital. Enya, Delta, Jaylynn, Kiara, and Katie as well as other people she barely knew visited and brought casseroles and other food so that she and her guys didn't have to cook.

Violet gazed at herself in the mirror as she washed her hands after using the facilities. Although the swelling was gone, there was still mottled hues of greens and yellows from her healing bruises on her jaw, cheek, and temple. While she hated that she and Cindy had been hurt, she was thankful they were both still alive.

Thankfully, other than Virgil slapping her around, Cindy had no other outward injuries and she hadn't been raped.

"Are you okay, sweetness?" Wilder asked as he entered the bathroom.

She turned toward him as she dried her hands and smiled. "I'm fine."

"Are you sure?" Cree asked.

He was leaning against the doorjamb and Nash was right behind him.

"Y'all need to stop fussing. The doctor's given me the all clear."

Wilder took a step closer, wrapped an arm around her waist, and pulled her up against him. "I love you so much, sweetness."

Violet cupped his cheek with her hand. "I love you, too, Wilder." She went up on tiptoes and kissed him lightly on the lips before lowering down again. She gazed at each of them for a moment and said, "Thank y'all for saving me and Cindy."

Cree and Nash moved further into the room.

Cree threaded his fingers with hers, brought her hand up to his mouth, and kissed the back of it. "You don't need to thank us, honey. We would and will do anything to keep you safe."

Nash moved in behind her and wrapped an arm around her shoulders and the top of her breasts. "We'd kill to protect you, baby. I love you so damn much, Violet." He kissed her bruised temple.

Violet leaned back against him and met his gaze over her shoulder. "I love you, too, Nash." She locked eyes with Cree. "I love you, Cree."

"You're my world, honey." Cree paused to clear his hoarse throat. "Please, promise us you'll never do anything like that again. I nearly lost it when I found out you were in danger."

"We all did," Wilder said.

"I never want to go through something like that ever, ever again," Nash whispered.

"Me either," Violet agreed.

Moving from NYC to Slick Rock had been a spur-of-the-moment decision all those months ago. She never would have thought the small, rural Colorado town and the people living in it would end up being her deliverance. And while she hoped that she was safe to live the rest of her life being happy with her men, she wouldn't change a thing if she could.

Wilder, Cree, and Nash had ended up rescuing her from the clutches of evil and given her freedom.

She was happy and in love, and now all she had to do was convince them that she was ready to make love with them again. She wanted, needed to feel their kisses, their touches, and their love emotionally as well as intimately. Having her men making love to her together would help her wipe away everything she had endured at the hands of a sick madman.

"Will you guys do something for me?" Violet asked.

"Anything," Wilder answered.

"Whatever you want, honey," Cree replied.

"Everything," Nash said with sincere conviction.

"Promise?" she asked.

"Yes," they answered at the same time without any hesitation and with a whole lot of trust.

Violet smiled, sidled out from between them, and walked toward the bedroom. She made sure to put an extra sway in her hips. She stopped beside the bed, keeping her back to her men, and quickly removed her T-shirt and shorts. Wilder groaned, Cree gasped, and Nash made a growly noise. She turned to face her men and said, "Please, make love with me."

As soon as Wilder nodded and tugged at his belt buckle, Cree and Nash moved faster than she'd ever seen them move before.

Violet giggled as she crawled up onto the bed after pulling the quilt down and then sat to watch the show. She was the one making sounds of desire as she stared at their sexy, naked, manly forms, and when Cree stepped closer, she wrapped her hand around his hard cock and pumped up and down.

She moaned when he threaded his fingers into her hair, and then she bent toward him.

Violet lapped at the bead of pre-cum and whimpered in need at his sweet-spicy taste. She opened her mouth and sank down over his hard dick.

"Fuck! Your mouth is heaven, honey."

"Speaking of honey," Wilder rasped out. "I need a taste."

Before she had time to blink, her hand was tugged from Cree's cock, and then he climbed onto the bed next to her. Nash got onto the mattress on the other side.

Violet was about to scoot up the bed since her legs were hanging over the end, but Wilder knelt, hooked his arms around her legs, and spread them wide before she could move.

"Oh," she moaned as he licked up through her folds before twirling his tongue over her clit.

Cree palmed a cheek, turned her face toward his, and slanted his mouth over hers. She moaned as their tongues dueled in an erotic dance of passion. Nash molded one breast and rolled the nipple while he suckled on the other one.

Violet's arousal went from simmering embers to a raging inferno.

Wilder stroked two fingers up into her pussy and pumped them in and out while laving and flicking his tongue over her clit.

The pressure grew fast, and before she knew it she was hovering right on the cusp of release. But she didn't want to come until she had her men deep inside of her. She turned her head to break the kiss with Cree, gasped in a lungful of air, and said, "Please."

Wilder lifted his head as he eased his fingers from her soaked pussy. He nodded at Cree and Nash. They tugged her further up the bed with a hand under each arm, and then Wilder got up on the mattress between her legs.

He nudged her thighs wider with a knee, clasped his erection in his hand, and then he was pushing inside of her. He groaned and ground his teeth, while she moaned.

Having her men make love to her was one of the most profound experiences of her life.

She shivered as her wet tissues stretched, and then she sighed when Wilder was in all the way. He blanketed her body with his, pushed an arm under her hips and another under her shoulders, and rolled until she was on top.

Violet bent her knees up, braced her hands on his chest, and then glanced at Cree. He already had the tube of lube in his hand, and she watched as he coated his hard, thick condom-covered cock with the viscous gel. Cree crawled down the bed and moved behind her.

She turned to face Nash and smiled when she noticed he was waiting for her, up on his knees just shy of her shoulders, and he was stroking his cock.

Violet curled her finger at him, beckoning him to come closer.

He shuffled a little toward her, and she brushed his hand away, wrapped her own around the base of his erection, and pumped him a few times. When he groaned, she leaned forward and took him into her mouth.

When Cree stroked a lubed finger over her star, she was the one moaning. She couldn't wait to be stuffed full by her men. She bobbed her head up and down Nash's cock, starting off slowly, wanting to make this last, so that they could all come together.

Cree rubbed the tip of his dick against her ass and then applied more pressure. Violet drew a deep breath in through her nose and then exhaled slowly the same way. She groaned as his cock eased in with a long slow stroke.

"Are you ready, baby?" Nash whispered in her ear, causing her to shiver and goose bumps to erupt over her whole body.

"Yes," she moaned.

Nash clasped her wrist and tugged her hand from around his cock. The hand in her hair tightened, heightening her arousal, and then he wrapped his own hand around the base of his dick.

"Let us do all the work, honey," Cree ordered.

She didn't even get to respond before they were all moving.

Cree drew out until just the tip of his erection was inside her ass, and as he drove back in, Wilder retreated from her pussy.

Nash began to rock his hips, gliding his hard dick in and out of her mouth, but not going in deep enough to choke or gag her with his hand in the way.

Violet burned from the inside out as they made love to her together. In and out they thrust into her mouth, ass, and pussy. Each heated stroke sent her another step up the steep slope until every muscle in her body was taut with tension.

When Wilder shoved a hand down between their bodies and started stroking her clit, Violet almost lost her mind.

The pressure grew as they pumped in and out, in and out, until she was a mindless being reaching for the stars.

And then the pressure burst.

She screamed as she started to come.

Violet's whole body shook and shivered while her internal muscles clenched and loosened, over and over.

"I'm gonna..." Nash groaned right before his cum spewed from the tip of his cock.

Violet gulped his delicious jism as she laved the underneath of his dick, hoping to enhance his climax. His dick twitched each time seed burst from it.

Seconds later Cree roared as he slammed deep into her ass, his erection juddering and jerking as he spent himself in her back channel.

Wilder gripped her hips firmly, his fingers digging into her skin, and he shouted as he surged deep into her pussy one last time. Aftershocks wracked her body as his dick pulsed and palpitated. Each time more of his essence spumed from his cock.

Violet slumped down onto Wilder's chest as she tried to regain her breath. Never in her life had she expected to ever love and find love with one man, let alone three, but she was so glad she had.

She was happy and content and looking forward to spending the rest of her life with the men who completed her.

* * * *

Violet sighed as she sank into the hot spa-bath water. Wilder, Cree, and Nash stepped into the tub and sat in the formfitting seats across from her. She frowned, because normally two of them sat on either side of her while she rested in the other's lap.

Wilder cleared his throat to garner her attention, and her frown deepened when she noticed one of his hands curled into a tight fist. He glanced at Cree and then Nash, and then they all shuffled toward her on their knees.

Cree laced his fingers with her right hand and Nash with her left.

Wilder rested a hand on her knee.

"Violet Evans, we love you more than we can ever say. You complete us when we didn't even know we weren't whole. You've delivered us from a life of loneliness. Would you please do us the honor of marrying us?"

Tears pooled in her eyes and spilled over her lower lids as the love and happiness in her heart overwhelmed her.

Violet didn't need to think about her answer in any way, shape, or form.

"Yes!" she said and then gasped as Wilder slid a diamond engagement ring on her finger.

As soon he was finished, she launched herself from her seat and straight into her men's arms, knowing they would catch her.

She was right where she was meant to be.

Violet's years of capture had ended up being her deliverance.

THE END

WWW.BECCAVAN-EROTICROMANCE.COM

Siren Publishing, Inc.
www.SirenPublishing.com

Lightning Source UK Ltd.
Milton Keynes UK
UKHW02f1233190218
318107UK00006B/1134/P